Kingdom of the Birds

Seppel and the Secret of the Wartburg Castle

HILDA DEMUTH-LUTZE

Kirk House Publishers
Minneapolis, Minnesota

Kingdom of the Birds
Seppel and the Secret of the Wartburg Castle
Hilda Demuth-Lutze

Copyright © 2010 Hilda Demuth-Lutze. All rights reserved.

Library of Congress Cataloging-in-Publication Data

Demuth-Lutze, Hilda.
  Kingdom of the birds : seppel and the secret of the Wartburg Castle /
Hilda Demuth-Lutze.
    p. cm.
  Includes bibliographical references.
  ISBN-13: 978-1-933794-26-6 (alk. paper)
  ISBN-10: 1-933794-26-7 (alk. paper)
  1. Luther, Martin, 1483-1546--Fiction. 2. Wartburg (Eisenach,
Germany)--Fiction. 3. Reformation--Germany--Fiction. I. Title.
  PS3604.E49K56 2010
  813'.6--dc22
                                        2010001849

Kirk House Publishers, PO Box 390759, Minneapolis, MN 55439
Manufactured in the United States of America

In memory of my son
Joseph,
a child of the Kingdom

Contents

CHAPTER 1

Faith and a Good Horse

To this day, whenever I smell the fragrance of apple blossoms, I remember that evening in the cottage many years ago. Mother and my three younger sisters and I huddled around the dying embers of the cooking fire. None of us dared to look at the empty chair beside the hearth. At the sound of footsteps in the yard, all of us turned toward the door. Little Annchen whispered, "Papa?" before Renata hushed her and Ludmilla began to cry again, her pale braids shaking as she sobbed.

My uncle walked in without knocking, as befit the owner of the tannery and the surrounding cottages. In the lantern light the scowling face under the dark hair looked like a ruined copy of Father's. Uncle Stefan stood silently in the doorway until Ludmilla stopped sniffling.

"I have buried my brother," he said, "and what has he left to me? A widow and four children."

Mother bent her head and pressed her lips against Annchen's curly head for a moment before she spoke. "Josef left you his share of the tannery. You know he worked hard to provide for us."

Uncle Stefan stared at me, "Or to pay school fees for a son fit for nothing but holding a broom."

"Please, Stefan," said Mother. "It was Josef's dearest wish to see our son attend a university. Seppel could become a scholar like your brother Spalatin—"

Uncle Stefan snorted, "Spalatin! What kind of name is that? The man names himself after our village but doesn't bother to return for his brother's funeral."

Renata pushed back her braids and lifted her chin. "Uncle Spalatin has many duties at the Saxon court. He's chaplain to Duke Frederick."

Ludmilla chimed in. "He chooses all the books for the Wittenberg library."

Uncle Stefan turned to me. "Almost grown, yet women and children must speak for you. A fine son indeed."

I could not meet his eyes, but I could feel him glaring down at me.

"Without your father in the tannery there is no money for schooling. Do you want your mother and sisters to go begging?"

I had to swallow hard before I could speak. "I will come to work for you."

"Your broom will be waiting."

The tannery stank. The process of turning animal skin into leather was an unpleasant business. Out in the yard, flies swarmed around fresh cowhides piled alongside the tanning vats, where an apprentice prodded the hides deep into the foul-smelling murk. Inside the dim tanning shed, flies buzzed around my ears as I stooped to sweep scraped hair from under a bench. Faintly I heard the bells of St. Nicholas summoning my old schoolmates. The boys would whisper until the priest entered the room, when they would open their Latin books and begin to work on translations.

At a thudding of hoofbeats I glanced out the doorway, squinting against the bright light as two horsemen entered the yard. From their richly-colored attire and gleaming swords I knew that the older horseman must be a knight and the younger his son or a squire.

The apprentice gaped at the horsemen.

"I seek Josef Burkhardt," said the knight.

The apprentice ducked his head respectfully. "He—he's dead, sir."

"Did he have a son?"

As the apprentice turned toward the doorway, I stepped outside, still holding the broom. "I'm Josef Burkhardt the Younger, sir."

The knight peered at me under grizzled brows, then pulled a small bundle from beneath his cloak. "I am Gottfried of Torgau, a friend of Spalatin. Your uncle asked me to deliver these letters to you." He thrust the bundle into my hands and said, "My squire and I will return for you when the sun is high. *Auf Wiedersehen.* Till we meet again."

"Return for me?"

But the two horsemen were already riding away down the lane, leaving me to stare at the folded papers in my hand.

Inside the cottage Mother turned the bundle over and over again, then handed it back to me. "You are still our scholar, Seppel. You will have to read for us."

I unfolded the wrapping to reveal two sealed letters. One was addressed to Josef Burkhardt of Spalt. As I broke the wax seal on that letter, Annchen ran her fingers over the writing on the other one. "Seppel, what does this say?"

"To Captain Hans von Berlepsch."

"Captain Hans von Berlepsch," Annchen echoed.

I read the first letter aloud as Renata and Ludmilla crowded in to peer at the elegant script.

> Wittenberg, Saxony
>
> 15 May 1521
>
> My dear nephew Josef,
>
> I am sorry that I am unable to return to Spalt to grieve with you and your family. Please convey my deepest sympathy to your mother and your sisters. Always remember your father as one who worked hard to serve God and his fellow man. There can be no higher tribute.
>
> I write to summon you to one year of service to his Electoral Grace, Duke Frederick of Saxony. Sir Gottfried will conduct you to your post in Thuringia.

I looked into my mother's startled eyes. I had never traveled farther than the Nuremberg market in our homeland of Franconia, and the border of Thuringia lay far to the north.

> You will report to Captain von Berlepsch, who will assign your duties in the name of his Grace. Please assure your mother that in recognition of your service, she and your sisters will be amply provided for.

"God be thanked," whispered Mother. Then her eyes filled with tears. "*Ach*, my dear son, how can I let you go?"

What would Mother and my sisters do without me? Who was this Captain von Berlepsch? Why should the Duke of Saxony concern himself about a Franconian village boy? Later that evening I watched

Mother run her hands over Father's well-worn saddlebag after she packed my few belongings and a loaf of bread. She drew a small pouch from beneath her apron, and I heard the clink of coins. "When you arrive at your destination," she said, "you must find a priest to say a Mass for your father's soul."

I shook my head. "You and the girls need the money."

"Who has greater need than a soul in purgatory?" Mother draped the cord of the pouch around my neck and pushed aside my fair hair to kiss my forehead. "You have always been a good son, Seppel. I know you will do what is right."

The next morning the bells of St. Nicholas were ringing when the two horsemen rode up to our cottage, a saddled horse trailing behind them. With the saddlebag slung over my shoulder, I watched Sir Gottfried dismount to greet my mother. Taking the reins of the saddled horse from the squire, the knight said to me, "As part of your recompense, you are to be given a suitable mount." Solemnly he handed me the reins.

My sisters clustered around the little black horse in delight. Ludmilla admired the dark eyes and patted the velvet muzzle. Annchen squealed when the horse snorted and tossed his head. Renata said boldly, "Sir, what is his name?"

The knight turned to the squire. "What do you call him, Erich?"

"Tintenfleck." The squire's voice was flat.

"Erich raised him from a colt," said Sir Gottfried. "Tintenfleck is well-broken and good-tempered. With the proper care he will serve for many years."

"Yes, sir." I glanced at the squire, whose face was sullen.

Sir Gottfried handed my mother a small bag of coins.

"Mama," said Annchen, "are we selling Seppel?"

"How can you say that?" Mother began to weep, and when my sisters saw her face, the three of them clung to me, sobbing while I tried to hold back my tears. I did not want the squire to see me cry.

On that first day of travel, I was not much of a horseman. Sir Gottfried showed me how to hold the reins and how to grip with my legs. He taught me to use the stirrups to ease Tintenfleck's jouncing trot, but my legs and backside were soon aching.

When we stopped at midday to rest the horses, Sir Gottfried seated himself under an oak tree, and the squire set out sausage and a wedge of cheese on a cloth before him. I stood beside the tethered horses until the knight called, "Come, young friend, and dine with us." I hesitated, then pulled the loaf from my saddlebag and carried it over to the tree. I unwrapped the bread and sat a respectful distance from the noblemen. Sir Gottfried cut a thick slice of the coarse brown bread and praised my mother's work. Erich did not touch my offering.

The evening shadows were long when we dismounted in the yard of a crossroads inn. Sir Gottfried said, "Always see to your horse's needs before you see to your own. Faith and a good horse will carry you far."

The knight entered the inn while the squire and I unsaddled the horses. I watched Erich rub down Sir Gottfried's horse with a bit of sacking. When he finished, he tossed the damp sacking to me and found a dry piece for his own mount. Briskly I began rubbing Tintenfleck's sweaty neck, humming a song my mother used to sing. The black ears flickered, whether in pleasure or annoyance I was not sure.

Then I followed Erich into the crowded inn, where we threaded our way through a noisy throng of merchants and drovers, noblemen and students. Sir Gottfried was sitting near the fireplace among several other men of rank. Erich directed me to a bench at the other end of the room, then joined the knight and his companions. After the long hours in the saddle, I was grateful to have a sturdy board beneath me. I leaned back, closed my eyes, and listened to the snatches of conversation in the room:

"*Gott im Himmel*, it's true. Luther has disappeared."

"Abducted, they say, by the pope's henchmen."

"Stabbed and left for dead in a silver mine."

"All that is known is that he was taken in the Thuringian Forest."

"God preserve the good *Herr Doktor*."

Drowsily I tried to remember what I knew of Martin Luther. The monk was a professor at the university in Wittenberg. He had become well known for writing against certain practices of the church. From the travelers' talk I learned that Luther's mysterious disappearance had occurred only days after he had defended his ideas before the emperor himself.

On the following evening as I rested my aching body in another crossroads inn, I heard even more astonishing rumors:

"Luther is being held for ransom by the emperor's agents."

"He has gone to raise an army to march against the pope."

"He was taken up to heaven like the prophet Elijah."

The next day we rode for hours through a dense forest. When the trail passed along a ridge overlooking a valley, Sir Gottfried pointed out a castle on a distant mountaintop, rising like an island in a sea of trees. "There is the Wartburg," he said. "We should arrive by nightfall."

I ventured to ask what had long been on my mind. "Sir, why would Duke Frederick send for me? What sort of duties might Captain von Berlepsch have for me?"

"I know no more than you, Burkhardt the Younger. Can you make music? Do you know your letters?"

Erich smirked. "Perhaps Duke Frederick had to send all the way to Franconia for a boy who can handle a broom."

CHAPTER 2

Within the Fortress

The Thuringian Forest was deep in shadows when Sir Gottfried and Erich and I reached the foot of the mountain. The knight called for us to dismount, and we led our tired horses up a dim path marked by the tracks of donkeys. I trudged along with my head down, staring at the grime-caked toes of my boots. At last Tintenfleck's hooves rang over wooden planks. I looked up from the drawbridge to see a stone archway over an enormous iron-clad door.

Within the great door, a smaller door creaked open. The noblemen's horses blocked my view, but I heard a deep voice say, "*Willkommen,* Sir Gottfried. Welcome to the Wartburg."

"Thank you, Otto. Is the Lord of Parrots expecting us?"

"Indeed, sir. Come in, come in."

The smaller door closed. With a rasp of metal, the great door swung open, and a flock of pigeons exploded in a whirring of wings. Tintenfleck and I followed the noblemen and their horses through a dark passageway into a narrow courtyard. The courtyard was flanked by the stone wall of the fortress on one side and a tall half-timbered building on the other.

Otto was a brawny soldier with a cheerful face. He bowed smartly to Erich. "Welcome to the Wartburg, sir." He seemed unsure how to address me, but then he said simply, "*Willkommen.*"

Another voice called across the courtyard. "Gottfried, you are as ugly as ever!" A bearded swordsman approached us.

The knight smiled. "And you, Hans, were never more charming."

The two men embraced, and the swordsman clapped Erich on the shoulder. Then he eyed me keenly. "Is this the boy?"

Sir Gottfried nodded. "This is young Burkhardt of Spalt."

Beside me the squire shifted his weight and scowled.

The knight said to me, "Give your message to Captain von Berlepsch."

I reached into the saddlebag for the letter.

The captain broke the seal, unfolded the paper, and read quickly. Then he stroked his beard. "Your uncle claims that you are honest, intelligent, and obedient."

"Y-yes, sir."

The captain thrust the letter into his sword belt. "I hope you will not prove him a liar." He whistled, and a boy trotted out of a stable. Then the captain said to Sir Gottfried, "Join me in the Ritterhaus. Tonight you share the hospitality of the Wartburg."

The stableboy took the reins of the noblemen's horses, but I held Tintenfleck's reins firmly. "I will see to my own horse."

Sir Gottfried chuckled and patted me on the shoulder. Behind his back Erich shot me a scornful glance.

In the stable I rewarded Tintenfleck with a thorough rubdown, giving myself over to the rhythm, the acrid smells of dander and sweat, the damp grittiness of the sacking. The stableboy watched me as he rubbed down the other horses. He must have wondered whether I should be shown the same respect as my companions. How exactly was I to fit into the world within these walls? I could not tell the stableboy that I was as mystified as he was.

I shouldered my saddlebag, taking comfort in the burden, and walked across the courtyard as if I were about to enter one more crossroads inn.

By the gleam of a lantern on a stone table I saw Otto sitting beside the door of the Ritterhaus. As I approached, he rose, picked up the lantern, and opened the door into a dark hallway. Lit by the swaying lantern, the shadows of stags' antlers and other hunting trophies seemed to writhe on the walls.

I heard quick footsteps on a stairway. A plump young woman in a cap and apron leaned over the banister. "What are you thinking, Otto? You must take the boy to the washhouse!"

"Yes, Hermina." The soldier's voice was surprisingly meek.

Otto led me down another passage to a small bare room. He poured water from a pitcher into a basin, and while I scrubbed my neck and arms, he cleaned my boots, shrugging off my embarrassed thanks.

Back in the entry hall the young woman was waiting for us. She crossed her arms and inspected me, her wide brown eyes seeming to miss nothing. At last she said pertly to Otto, "You are dismissed."

Otto grinned, bowed more deeply to her than he had to the noblemen, and left the hall.

The young woman said, "You look much more presentable now."

"Thank you, good *Frau*."

She smiled. "You may call me Hermina."

"I'm Seppel."

"Please come with me, Seppel."

Slightly comforted by hearing the familiar name, I followed Hermina up the stairs and stood behind her while she rapped on a door and listened to an answering voice within. Hermina opened the door to reveal Sir Gottfried and Captain von Berlepsch seated before a fireplace, each holding a tankard in his hand.

The captain set down his tankard. "That will be all, Hermina. Come here, young Burkhardt of Spalt."

As I stood before him, he said slowly, "Now tell me the truth. For what purpose did Spalatin send you here?"

"He told me nothing, sir," I said in confusion. "He wrote only that you would assign my duties."

The captain glanced at the knight. "For a commoner, Spalatin plays a courtier's game remarkably well." He turned back to me. "Sit down, young Burkhardt. There in the corner."

I was grateful to rest my legs and relieved that the captain did not question me further.

Instead he addressed Sir Gottfried. "Tell me, what is the latest news of Luther? At the Wartburg we hear very little of the outside world."

I listened to the knight repeat the stories we had heard during our journey.

Captain von Berlepsch smiled at some accounts but then became somber. "I fear the worst," he said, "but one must hope for the best. In this part of the empire the *Herr Doktor* Luther has more friends than enemies."

Sir Gottfried raised his tankard. "Thanks to Martin Luther, the pope will no longer fill his coffers with Saxon gold."

"Or Thuringian silver," said the captain.

The two men went on to speak of alliances and skirmishes among various princes of the empire. They seemed to have forgotten my presence. I leaned back and shut my eyes. The warmth of the fire lulled me, and the voices became a current of sound flowing over me.

I dimly remember being guided out of the room. "God be with you, Burkhardt the Younger," a gruff voice whispered. *"Auf Wiedersehen."*

I woke with a start, my ears ringing, and sat up in a strange bed, clutching the pouch around my neck. Where was I, and what was that shrill noise? At last my panic subsided enough that I recognized the clamor as the calling of hundreds, perhaps thousands, of birds.

On the floor beside the bed lay my saddlebag. I reached down to touch the leather, assuring myself that it was real. Then I pushed aside the fine coverlet and walked over to the window, where light shone through waves and bubbles frozen within circles of glass. I tugged at the latch, and the window swung open. Instantly the bird calls grew louder.

Beyond the mountaintop castle the vast forest stretched to the horizon. I leaned over the wide sill and saw treetops far below the steep drop of the mountain.

A rap at the door startled me, and I slammed the window shut.

"Good morning, Seppel," called a cheerful female voice. "The captain is waiting to see you."

I straightened my rumpled tunic and sat down to put on my boots.

When I opened the door, Hermina looked me up and down, her pretty mouth puckered into a frown. "I hope the clothes fit," she murmured.

She led me past several closed doors and down the stairs to the entry hall. Opening the door to the courtyard, she said, "Ask the cook for a bowl before you see the captain." Hermina pointed to a cobblestone path beyond the stone table. "The kitchen is over there. Don't mind Gunda's temper. She's forever threatening to chop Dolf into pieces."

I walked down the path and stood outside the kitchen, listening to bellowed curses and a great clatter of metal. A shaggy-haired boy bolted through the door, almost flattening me, and then I found myself gazing at an apron spattered with grease and blood. A muscular arm brandished a cleaver a few inches from my ear. "Worthless scullion!" I looked up into the flaring nostrils of a scowling face. A giant of a woman glared down at me. "What are you staring at?"

"If you please, *Frau* Gunda," I stammered, "Hermina sent me to ask for something to eat."

The woman pushed back her kerchief and wiped her forehead with the back of one large hand. "Why do fools make my work so difficult?"

I did not know how to answer that.

The cook turned away and buried the tip of the cleaver in a chopping block. Wiping her hands on her apron, she strode to an enormous hearth and ladled stew from a iron pot into a wooden bowl. "Take it and be gone."

I stepped forward cautiously and took the steaming bowl from her hand. "Thank you, good *Frau*." I backed away slowly, as one might in the presence of royalty or a dangerous animal.

"Boy!"

"Yes, *Frau*?"

"Don't forget the bread."

I carried the bowl and a thick wedge of bread to the edge of the courtyard, where I sat with my back against a blossoming pear tree. The stew was brimming with chunks of meat, and I sopped up the savory juices with the rich dark crust of the bread.

Licking my fingers, I took my first look at the castle grounds by daylight. Through an archway I could glimpse a second courtyard flanked by ancient stone buildings and square towers.

A pair of soldiers emerged from the Ritterhaus and entered the underpass that led to the castle gate. Alongside the kitchen an old man was repairing a fence around a garden plot. Nearby, a little girl scattered grain to ducks and geese squabbling greedily at her feet. From the stable I heard the nickering of horses. With a guilty start I rose to my feet. Why had I not looked in on faithful Tintenfleck?

As I walked toward him, I saw that the adjoining stalls were empty. A jolt of despair left me as breathless as if I just had been kicked. Sir Gottfried and his squire had already departed, abandoning me to this strange new world. I brushed past Tintenfleck's hindquarters and wrapped my arms tightly around his neck, pressing my cheek against the thick black mane.

CHAPTER 3

The Family von Berlepsch

"Boy. Boy!"

I raised my head from Tintenfleck's neck to see a young woman with narrowed eyes and a sullen mouth.

"Fetch Eisblume's saddle and bridle."

I did not question the order. I patted Tintenfleck and slipped out of the stall. At one end of the stable a row of bridles hung above an assortment of saddles. I hesitated, then chose the finest bridle and the daintiest saddle to carry down the aisle.

Without a word the young woman took the bridle and slipped the bit deftly into the mouth of a white horse. She backed the horse out of the stall and signaled me to lift the saddle into place. When I fumbled with the girth strap, she tossed back long braids and said, "What kind of stableboy are you? Eisblume cannot bear clumsiness."

I retreated, burning with shame.

The young woman led her horse to a mounting block beside the stable door. Sunlight turned her hair a fiery red, and I glimpsed dark boots under the green gown as she gathered her skirts, stepped onto the block, and swung into the saddle.

The white horse trotted briskly around the yard, and then the young woman halted outside the Ritterhaus and called loudly, "Otto! Otto, where are you? Saddle up. I wish to ride!"

The soldier appeared at a door near the underpass. "I'm sorry, *Fräulein*. I cannot accompany you this morning."

The rider glanced at me. "Then let the stableboy accompany me, if he happens to know how to sit a horse."

"That is no stableboy, *Fräulein*, and he is not free to ride. Your father has business with him."

"Then I will ride alone. Open the gate."

"You know I cannot do that, *Fräulein*. Your father will not permit it."

The rider dug her heels into her horse's flanks and began to race around the yard, turning left and right in a dizzying series of figure eights between the castle wall and the Ritterhaus. I watched in wonder, unable to understand how she signaled the horse. I could not imagine making such quick turns or staying in the saddle if I did.

Otto beckoned me. "The captain wishes to see you in the gateroom."

I hurried over the cobblestones, still fascinated by the frenzied circling of the rider on the white horse. Otto led me up a flight of stairs to a room directly over the entrance to the castle.

Captain von Berlepsch was alone in the room. "That will be all, Otto."

The soldier bowed and closed the door.

The room was sparsely furnished with several benches surrounding a long table, piled with rolled documents. The stone walls were bare except for a row of shields. In one corner a green parrot on a tall perch cocked its head and eyed me suspiciously.

The captain stared at me for an uncomfortably long time before he spoke. "Have you any idea where you are?" He pushed aside some of the papers on the table and uncovered a large map.

I peered at the intricately drawn world before me. Tiny clusters of rooftops indicated the towns, while churches and castles were delicately outlined, and blue-tinted lines showed rivers and streams among a green-tinted forest. Near a town labeled "Eisenach," I found the outline of a castle marked "The Wartburg." I could have held the castle in the palm of my hand, as if it were the hand of God.

"Here," I said, careful not to let my finger touch the map.

The captain pointed to a quill pen beside an inkwell and pushed a scrap of parchment closer to me. "Write a few words for me."

I dipped the quill into the well and brushed off the excess ink before I touched the nib to the page. The captain leaned forward as the quill moved over the paper.

An unearthly screech shattered the quiet of the room, and I spattered ink over the table. In fright I stared at the parrot in the corner.

"Pay no attention to Master Klüglein," said the captain. "Keep writing."

I obeyed quickly, not stopping to think what I should write.

"The hand of God is leading the Lord of Parrots." The captain looked at me sharply. "What does that mean?"

"I don't know, sir. The words just came into my head."

"Do you know why I am called the Lord of Parrots?"

"No, sir."

"Look there." The captain pointed toward the wall, where the design on the center shield featured five green parrots on a field of gold. "I bear arms in the service of the Elector Frederick, Duke of Saxony and Landgrave of Thuringia. To fulfill my duty, I must be assured of the loyalty of those I command. Do I make myself clear?"

"Yes, sir."

"When a new man is placed under my command, I must know that he will obey my orders without question. Is that clear?"

"Yes, sir."

The captain turned to the door. "Otto! We are ready for you."

The soldier entered, holding a gleaming pair of shears.

"Your first duty, young Burkhardt," said the captain, "is to look and act as if you are of noble rank."

"Why must I do that, sir?"

"Have you already forgotten that you are not to question me?" The captain pointed to a bench. "Sit there, and let Otto do his work."

I sat absolutely still while the blades of the shears glinted alongside my face. Locks of fair hair fell into my lap. My nose itched, but I did not dare to sneeze. At last Otto told me to stand up and helped me brush off the hair clinging to my tunic and breeches.

"Now take him to the washhouse. Bring him back when he smells less like a peasant."

In the washhouse Otto and I met Hermina, who was pouring water from a steaming kettle into a large washtub. On a bench lay fine linens, a russet tunic, leggings, and a gilt-trimmed cape.

I looked dubiously at the tub.

Otto grinned. "Take everything off, and scrub yourself well." He tossed me a cloth, and then he and Hermina left me alone.

I remember how miserable I felt, crouching naked in the tub, still trying to figure out why I had been brought to this strange place. After I dried myself and dressed in the new clothes, the little pouch on the cord around my neck was all that remained of my life in Spalt. As I followed Otto back to the gateroom, I wondered how I would find a priest to say that Mass for Father.

Captain von Berlepsch said, "Now let me see you cross the room like a nobleman's son."

Feeling ridiculous, I walked across the slate floor. The green parrot cocked its head and eyed me balefully.

"*Bei allen Heiligen!*" said the captain. "You walk as if you are carrying a broom, not a sword."

"Sir, I don't know how to carry a sword."

"You will learn, young Burkhardt. You will learn."

The captain began to pace the room. "At all times you must remember that your family belongs to the nobility. Those who have power over you demand your loyalty. Those over whom you have power depend upon your justice. You and your father and his father before him are the knights who protect the German people and keep the German lands secure."

He halted and looked me over. "Your stance is now adequate, but a young lord would not look so eager to please. Remember that you are superior to everyone of common blood."

I pictured the squire Erich, who always seemed about to sneer. I tried to shape my mouth like his.

The captain snorted. "Are you sick to your stomach?"

Feeling even more foolish, I tried to imitate the expression I had seen on the rider of the white horse.

"Good!" said the captain. "That is exactly right." He strode to the door and shouted for Hermina, then turned to me. "When you meet a woman of the nobility, you must show the utmost respect. Bow from the waist. So."

The captain's bow was supple and elegant. He was light on his feet, as if he kept time to some internal music. "Never presume to touch a lady unless she first extends her hand to you."

Hermina hurried into the gateroom. "Does everything fit, sir? The tunic may be too long, as we didn't know what to expect. I could shorten it if—"

"The fit is good. Stand beside me and pretend to be Lady von Berlepsch."

"Oh, sir! What do you mean, sir?"

"I did not ask you to pretend to be stupid. Stand still and hold out your hand."

"Yes, sir." Hermina obeyed, pink with embarassment.

The captain placed the tips of his fingers just under her fingertips and swept a bow. "Gracious lady, I am most pleased to make your acquaintance."

Hermina raised her other hand to stifle a laugh.

The captain rose from his bow. "A lady of the nobility would never giggle."

"I beg your pardon, sir."

After the captain pronounced my manners adequate, he ordered Hermina to take me back to the Ritterhaus to meet the family von Berlepsch. Trying not to squirm inside in the stiff new clothing, I followed Hermina down a passageway. I could hear the music of a stringed instrument playing a dance tune at a frantic tempo, over and over again.

When Hermina and I appeared in the doorway, the music stopped. Hermina bobbed a curtsey and said, "Lady von Berlepsch, Dame Adela, and *Fräulein* Ilse, I present Josef Burkhardt of Franconia."

I bowed deeply from the waist. "Gracious ladies, I am most pleased to make your acquaintance."

When I straightened up, I saw a fair-haired noblewoman reclining upon a couch. She was wrapped in an embroidered coverlet in spite of the warmth of the room. On a straight-backed chair beside her sat an older woman dressed in gray, a length of tapestry in her lap. The older woman lowered her needle and stared at me. Except for the lace draped over her silver hair, everything about her was sharp—her eyes, her cheekbones, her chin. Across the room a young woman holding a lute rose from a cushioned window seat, and I glimpsed dainty slippers under a green gown.

The older woman spoke. "You may go, Hermina. Come here, young man." Even her voice was sharp. I walked slowly forward, and the fair-haired woman on the couch held out her hand. She was thin and pale with dark shadows in the hollows under her eyes. When I placed my fingertips just underneath hers, I could see blue lines under the translucent skin.

"Josef, I hope you enjoy your stay at the Wartburg," Lady von Berlepsch said.

"Thank you, my lady."

Dame Adela turned to the window, the movement abrupt and birdlike. "Ilse, come to greet our guest."

Not until the young woman stood before me, eyes lowered, did I notice that her crown of braids was a fiery red. I could hardly believe that this meek creature was the rider of the white horse.

I bowed. *"Fräulein* Ilse, I am most pleased to make your acquaintance."

When I rose and looked into those green eyes, I saw no hint that we had ever met.

Ilse said softly, "The pleasure is entirely mine."

CHAPTER 4

Of Lute and Sword

Dame Adela said, "Sit down, Josef." With her chin she indicated a chair beside a small table.

I walked across the patterned carpet, conscious of the eyes of the three women upon me, remembering too late that I should look confident. When I sat down, my elbow bumped the table, rattling carved figures on a board of inlaid wood squares. Guiltily I drew my arms in and sat stiffly in the chair.

Still holding the neck of the lute, Ilse slid into a chair on the other side of the table. With her free hand she touched one of the figures. "Do you play?"

"No, *Fräulein*."

The green eyes opened wide. "How very odd. I thought everyone of noble birth would know the game of chess."

I could think of no response to this remark.

Lady von Berlepsch roused herself enough to say, "Play us another tune, Ilse. Something soothing, if you please."

Ilse sighed and took the lute onto her lap, setting her fingers to the strings. She plucked out a melody I recognized, a cheerful song of springtime. Lady von Berlepsch hummed along, her own fingers moving as if touching invisible strings. I relaxed slightly in my chair. How good to know that the residents of a castle could enjoy the same music as the villagers back in Spalt.

After the last notes died away, Ilse held out the lute. "Now it's your turn."

"I—I don't know how to play."

"How surprising." Her voice was like a cat's purr. "Here in Thuringia everyone of noble birth learns the lute."

Lady von Berlepsch said gently, "Perhaps things are different in Franconia."

Dame Adela's needle stabbed the tapestry. "A great Franconian musician is well-known at the Wartburg."

Striving for an intelligent reply, I said, "Does he come here often?"

Ilse's eyebrows rose. "Not for the past three hundred years."

Lady von Berlepsch smiled. "Surely you've heard of Wolfram von Eschenbach."

"Oh yes, my lady." The minstrel's name was as welcome as a friend among strangers. Our village musicians played his songs, and Mother sang them at home.

Dame Adela lifted her sharp chin. "He was one of the contestants in the Tournament of Song at the Wartburg. My ancestors were among those present."

Ilse said rapidly, as if parroting the words. "Dame Adela is a descendant of Thuringian royalty, related by blood to Saint Elisabeth herself."

Dame Adela frowned. "Royal lineage is not to be mocked. For a young woman named after the sainted Elisabeth, you are sadly lacking in her fine qualities."

Ilse sniffed. "I have no desire to become a saint."

"You are in no danger of that, my girl."

The lute thunked to the floor, and Ilse said, "Neither are you."

Dame Adela glared at her.

Lady von Berlepsch crossed herself. "Ilse, you must ask forgiveness of Our Blessed Mother. Ask Saint Elisabeth to give you strength to control your temper."

Hermina's voice at the door was a welcome relief. "If you please, my ladies," she said, "the captain has asked to see young Burkhardt."

I rose and bowed deeply as before, then followed Hermina to the front hall. Glancing around to make sure we were alone, I said, "Why does the captain want me to make this pretense?"

"It's not our place to question him." Hermina bit her lip. "Also, you must remember that the castle servants are beneath your notice."

"Even you and Otto?"

She smiled. "Of course not. Otto and I are servants of the family von Berlepsch."

Otto was waiting for me at the stone table outside the Ritterhaus. He led me under the arch to the inner courtyard. Gaping at the ancient stone palace and the soaring square towers, I said, "Who lives in the palace?"

Otto shrugged. "Mostly pigeons."

At a large cistern I put my hands on the mossy rim and peered down into the water. Against a bright circle of sky I saw a worried youth with blonde bangs cut in a precise line across his forehead.

"Young Burkhardt!"

The captain glared at me from the other side of the cistern. "What are you gawking at? We have work to do in the armory."

On the far side of the courtyard, Otto opened a door, and I followed Captain von Berlepsch into a dim high-ceiling chamber full of weapons and armor and chain mail. A row of helmets lined a ledge above a row of shields. On the walls hung swords and pikes and battle-axes. The captain led me to an enormous fireplace, where blades of various sizes lay on a long table.

"Had you been born into my world," he said, "the names of these weapons would have been among your first words. You and I have a long way to go."

He picked up a short two-edged blade with a simple crossguard hilt. "This is an arming sword. I hang this from my belt." He pointed to a heavier weapon with a blade about four feet long. "The longsword I hang from my saddle."

The captain showed me daggers and dusacks, war hammers and lances, maces and flails. He told me to run my hands over the blade of the halberd, a gigantic axe crowned with a spear point on a six-foot pole. "With this weapon a skilled warrior can cleave plate armor."

I did not like to think about the ways in which such weapons were used. Back in Spalt, the other boys and I used to play at combat, brandishing sticks and shouting threats, but this grim machinery of war stirred queasiness in my belly.

Captain von Berlepsch slid the halberd back onto its hook on the wall. "Let me see your stance."

I was not sure what he meant, so I tried to stand straight and tall. The captain circled me slowly, watching me out of the corner of his eye. Abruptly he sidestepped, shoving me so hard that I staggered and fell.

He reached out a strong hand and pulled me to my feet. When I winced and rubbed my backside, he smiled. "As the fightmasters say, *Was sehrt, das lehrt.* What hurts, teaches. You were too easily thrown off balance. A fighter must stay balanced, like a pair of scales."

Dutifully I imitated his stance, knees slightly bent, shoulders forward, and elbows out.

The captain drew his sword and stood facing me, the blade mere inches from my throat. Trying not to flinch, I hoped that the next lesson would prove less painful than the first.

With the point of the sword, the captain traced a cross over my tunic, one line from neck to crotch, the other from arm to arm. Then he tapped each of the quarters and said, "These are the four openings."

The blade touched the upper right square of the invisible diagram. "Of course, the spot you aim for in your opponent is the one you protect most fiercely in yourself. Again, balance is all."

Captain von Berlepsch sheathed his weapon and picked up the smaller of two wooden swords. Holding the blade, he extended the hilt to me. With a trace of a smile he said, "Use it wisely and well."

Over the next hour I fell on my backside twice more. My arms ached from holding the sword at an exact height and precise angle. More than once I was slapped by the flat of the captain's wooden sword or bruised by the blunt end. Captain von Berlepsch had numerous ways of reminding me not to leave myself open to attack. One time I yelped when his blade caught me smartly across the ribcage. The lesson ended with a slashing cross cut that made the air hum. My wooden sword clattered on the slate floor. I stood breathing heavily, staring at my lost weapon.

"You have much to learn about the knightly arts," said the captain. "Still, I am convinced that the task is not impossible."

I raised my head. "You can't possibly hope to convince anyone that I am anything but a peasant."

"I do not intend to present you at court."

"Your own daughter knows how ignorant I am."

The captain's eyes narrowed. "What my daughter knows does not concern you. Follow me."

He walked out of the armory so fast that I had to trot to keep up. Outside the kitchen he halted so abruptly that I almost bumped into him.

"Gunda!"

The cook appeared in the doorway, wiping flour-coated hands on her greasy apron.

"Prepare a tray for Sir Georg at once."

Frau Gunda muttered something that Captain von Berlepsch chose to regard as consent.

He turned to me. "Bring the tray to the gateroom. You will meet the knight whom you are being trained to serve."

He strode away, leaving me to puzzle over what I had just heard.

"So you are to meet the mysterious Sir Georg." The kitchen boy peered around the corner, his blue eyes half-hidden by tangled dark hair. "No one but the captain has seen him. Hermina says he has a horrible disease and nobody dares to go near." The boy sidled closer. "I heard Otto say that Sir Georg is tormented by demons."

I did not know how to respond. Hermina had told me that the servants of the castle should be beneath my notice, but how could I possibly ignore such remarks?

There came a crash of metal and a bellow from the kitchen. "Dolf, when I find you, I will boil you in a cauldron!"

Instantly the kitchen boy vanished.

I walked over to the pear tree under which I had eaten my morning meal. Those few hours seemed a lifetime away. The kitchen boy's words kept spinning in my head. What manner of man was this knight? Was I destined to serve a leper or a madman? Surely my uncle would not knowingly place me in danger. Yet how could a chaplain at the Saxon court understand what was happening in a faraway Thuringian castle?

"Boy!"

I leaped to my feet and hurried to the kitchen. The cook jerked her chin toward a covered dish on a tray, then turned away. As I picked up the tray, I reflected that I was better suited for kitchen duties than for the knightly arts.

I entered the Ritterhaus by the side door, where Otto stood holding a covered tankard. He placed the tankard on the tray, and we climbed the stairs to the gateroom.

Captain von Berlepsch was waiting for us. Silently he stepped across the hall to a door that was barred and chained. From a ring of keys he selected one to insert into the heavy lock. Otto loosed the chain and lifted the iron-plated bar.

The captain turned to me. "Sir Georg's room is at the end of the hall. Ask him no questions, and do not weary him with your presence."

"Yes, sir." I had no wish to remain long in the company of the unfortunate prisoner.

Otto pulled open the door. Ahead rose a dark and narrow staircase that turned sharply, revealing only a blank wall.

"Go now," said the captain. "Your lord is waiting."

I steadied the tray and stepped forward. The door swung shut behind me.

CHAPTER 5

The Mysterious Knight

The steps were uneven, and the way dark. My fear that I might stumble and upset the tray was nearly as great as my dread of the unknown man above. I reached the top of the staircase and walked down a narrow hall to an open door, where I halted so abruptly that the covered dish rattled. The sound did not seem to disturb the man inside the small chamber, who sat with his back to the door. He appeared to be writing. A sheathed sword lay on the slate floor beside his chair. The man was clad in scarlet, and his black hair was close-cropped, as if his head had once been shaved because of disease.

Nerving myself not to flinch at any horrible pockmarks or scars, I said, "If you please, Sir Georg, I have brought your evening meal."

The chair legs scraped across the slate, and the knight turned to me, quill in hand.

I remember vividly my first sight of that face. Sir Georg was no monster after all. Above a new beard bristling over a square jaw, his features were rugged but not ugly. Deep-set dark eyes stared at me so intently that I wondered if Dolf was right and the man was indeed mad.

At last the knight spoke. "Forgive my wonder. Many days have passed since I saw a young face." He set down his quill without taking his eyes from me. "Are you the captain's son?"

"No, sir."

"What does your mother call you?"

"Seppel, sir."

"For Josef, of course. A fine biblical name. I am called Georg. After the dragon-slayer, they tell me." He rose suddenly and walked to the window, where the bull's-eye glass panes stood open to the evening breeze. "I am named for a champion, yet I sit here in idleness while a great dragon ravages the land. The wicked have drawn their swords and bent their bows to slay the upright."

His words were very strange, and his expression was fierce. I wondered whether I should leave him alone with his troubled thoughts.

Sir Georg turned to me. "But their swords shall enter into their own hearts, and their bows shall be broken. Thus it has been written."

"Yes, sir." I looked about for a place to set the tray so I could leave as quickly as possible. The table was covered with loose papers and a few bound volumes.

Sir Georg's face changed. "Let me make a place for that." He collected the papers from the table and piled them on the floor, anchoring the stack neatly with his sword.

I set down the tray. "Will you require anything else of me, sir? Captain von Berlepsch said I was to serve as your page."

"Did he indeed?" The knight's hearty laugh was as unexpected as the earlier flash of anger. "I have little need of a sword-polisher. Yet I welcome your company." He fetched a stool from the corner. "Come, young friend, break bread with me." He sat down beside me, closed his eyes, and bowed his head.

To this day I remember how that simple table prayer affected me. The knight spoke as if the Lord Jesus himself sat at the table among us.

I opened my eyes, and the knight lifted the cover of the dish to reveal a roast fowl and an array of dried fruits on a trencher of brown bread.

"My host treats me well," said Sir Georg. "He keeps a fine cook and provides excellent beer." He took a long drink from the tankard.

It seemed odd for a prisoner to speak so cheerfully of his warden. The ways of the nobility were strange indeed.

Sir Georg broke off a glaze-crusted drumstick and invited me to do the same. "Now, Seppel, I have heard enough to know that you are no Thuringian. Where is your home?"

"In Franconia near Nuremberg." Afraid the knight would realize I was not of noble birth, I added quickly, "And where is your home, sir?" Too late I remembered the captain's warning.

My question did not seem to offend Sir Georg. "Most recently I lived in Saxony, and now I am an exile in the Kingdom of the Birds." He raised his tankard in a salute to the open window, through which we could hear the evening calls of the forest. "Today I caught the scent of blossoms. Tell me what is flowering out there."

"The orchards are in bloom, sir."

"I fear I shall not see the flowers," said the knight, "but perhaps I will enjoy the fruit."

So many questions whirled in my mind. What had this man done to deserve punishment? How long had he been imprisoned?

Sir Georg finished off the last of the roast fowl and offered thanks again to God. "How pleasant it is to have a companion. If you are willing and the captain permits, I hope you will always dine with me."

I carried the tray down the narrow staircase. Otto must have been standing guard, for the door opened as I turned the last corner. In the gateroom the captain sat with a tankard close at hand. The green parrot screeched and flapped its wings.

"Sir Georg wishes me to take my meals with him," I said.

The captain stroked his beard. "A good arrangement. Otherwise I would have to seat you with my household."

I was glad the knight's invitation saved me from dining with Ilse von Berlepsch.

The captain said, "And how did my guest enjoy his meal?"

"Why do you call him a guest, sir? He's a prisoner." Instantly I regretted the words.

The captain frowned. "I need not explain myself to a peasant boy."

I slunk down the stairs after Otto, waiting till we were out in the courtyard to ask, "Why is Sir Georg a prisoner? What crime has he committed?"

Otto shook his head. "It's not our place to question such things. Perhaps he has offended someone of great rank."

"How long will he be locked in that room?"

Otto shrugged. "Who can say?" He lowered his voice. "You must watch your tongue. The captain has little patience for those who challenge him."

I sat under the pear tree and thought about the knight who would never see these blossoms. With a rustling of leaves and creaking of branches, the kitchen boy dropped to the grass beside me.

"Is he quite horrible?" Dolf's pale eyes were wide. "Did he rave and froth at the mouth?"

"Don't be foolish. He appears perfectly ordinary."

Dolf pushed back his shaggy hair and crept closer. "What do you mean?"

I eyed him coldly. "I need not explain myself to a kitchen boy."

When I retired to my chamber that night, I knelt at the window and tried to pray the way Sir Georg did, as if our Lord were in the room beside me. Instead of feeling the presence of God, I kept recalling the events of my first day at the Wartburg. Staring at the linked circles of glass, I pictured a succession of faces and heard the steely voice of the captain, the simmering rage of the cook, the honey-coated resentment of Ilse. The faces and voices were clear, but my own purpose in this castle was as dark as the night beyond the window.

When I fell at last into a restless sleep, Captain von Berlepsch rose up before me, sword in hand, striking Sir Georg again and again while the knight tried in vain to parry the blows with a goosefeather quill. Above them flew the green parrot, screeching *"Was sehrt, das lehrt! Was sehrt, das lehrt!"*

CHAPTER 6

Circles in the Yard

By the time the pear blossoms withered and fell, I had become accustomed to my daily routine at the Wartburg. Sir Georg seemed to spend most of his waking hours writing. I learned to gauge his mood by standing outside the door with my tray before I announced myself.

On some days I heard the knight's voice in the chamber before I reached the doorway. Muttering aloud, often in Latin, he would pace the floor like a chained bear I had seen in Nuremberg. Back and forth, back and forth went the footsteps of the prisoner, from table to window to door. On such days he paid little attention to his meal, sometime signaling me to set down the tray and leave him alone.

On other days Sir Georg would invite me to enter but would remain intent upon his work. I would sit patiently on the stool, balancing the tray on my knees, listening to the calling birds outside the window and the scratching of the quill. At last the knight would set aside his pages and turn to me. "So, my dear Seppel, what has the delightful Gunda provided for us today?"

My visits with the imprisoned knight were more satisfying than my sessions with the family von Berlepsch. As part of my schooling in the knightly arts, the captain ordered me to spend a few hours with the noblewomen every day. How I wished I could have enjoyed the company of Otto or Hermina instead of maintaining this pretense!

"Ilse," said Lady von Berlepsch one afternoon, "your father wishes you to teach Josef to play the lute."

Ilse eyed me skeptically. "I can teach only by example." She set her fingers to the strings and played a tune so fast that no dancer could have kept the tempo. Then she handed me the lute. "Try that."

Dame Adela clicked her tongue. "You will never get a husband unless you display more humility."

Ilse scowled. "I'm not interested in getting a husband."

Dame Adela sniffed. "Even young Peter of Castle Altenstein may lose interest if you insist on besting him at everything."

Lady von Berlepsch cut in smoothly. "Bring me the lute, Josef, and sit here beside me."

I sat stiffly on the couch, conscious of Ilse's displeasure, while Lady von Berlepsch showed me how to hold the lute and guided my hands on the strings. "There, you see? Pluck a low string and then a high. Again, please. You must use the soft of your fingers, not the nails, for the sweetest sound."

My nearness to the lady allowed me to see just how very frail she was, so thin her hands seemed as delicate as a bird's claws. The bluish shadows were ever present under her eyes, and at times her breathing became suddenly quick and then slowed once more.

"The lute has a beautiful voice," said Lady von Berlepsch, "but you must coax her to speak."

Remembering the echoing birdsong in the forest, I played a simple sequence again and again, striving to summon the voice of the lute.

"Excellent. Do you hear him, Ilse? He plays with such feeling."

Ilse did not respond.

I flexed my aching fingers and shrugged off the lady's expression of sympathy by murmuring, *"Was sehrt, das lehrt."*

Lady von Berlepsch burst into a peal of laughter. "So exactly like the captain!" Then the laughter turned to coughing. Her hoarse rasping rang out over the room. Alarmed, I rose from my seat, still clutching the lute.

Dame Adela pushed me aside and seated herself beside Lady von Berlepsch. "There, there," she said, as if soothing a child. "Breathe deeply now. Be still, my dear, be still."

At last the lady was able to catch her breath, but then another spasm of coughing seized her. Dame Adela signaled me to leave the room.

I set down the lute and turned to go.

Ilse hissed, "How dare you cause my mother such pain?"

Escaping as quickly as I could, I wandered blindly through the Ritterhaus until I found Hermina bustling about the dining hall. With a glance at the door, I said, "Is Lady von Berlepsch very ill?"

"She suffers greatly." Hermina lowered her voice. "Ilse was her first child and her last. The poor captain has no son to carry on his name."

I understood that this was a terrible thing for a nobleman.

Hermina draped the cloth over the table and placed candlesticks neatly at either end. "Ilse is of an age to marry, but the captain has not yet arranged a betrothal. The lady cannot bear to let her daughter go. When Ilse leaves the Wartburg, Lady von Berlepsch may never see her again in this world."

One day the captain took me to the stable, where he watched me saddle Tintenfleck. "Sir Gottfried taught you well," he said. I was pleased on behalf of the knight who had brought me to the castle. But when I mounted my horse and rode around the yard, the captain's expression changed. "You look like a plow boy after a day in the field. Stop clutching the saddle. Shoulders back, chin up."

He put Tintenfleck on a long lead line and made me drop the reins. Then he ordered me to cross my arms and take my feet out of the stirrups so that I could grip only with my legs.

When Captain von Berlepsch urged the horse into a trot, I tried not to react to the pounding of the saddle against my backside. Then the captain halted Tintenfleck so suddenly that I was nearly catapulted over my horse's head.

"*Bei allen Heiligen!* Didn't you see his ears flicker when I tugged on the line? A horseman must be vigilant."

The captain shouted across the yard, "Otto! Fetch my daughter." Then he turned again to me. "Once more at a trot. And this time you are to remember that a horse is not a hay wagon."

Dutifully I watched Tintenfleck's ears and tried to judge when he was likely to change his gait.

"Better," said the captain. He halted the horse and allowed me to take up my reins.

A door of the Ritterhaus opened. Gathering up her skirts, Ilse fairly flew across the yard, her face alight with pleasure. "I'm ready, Father! Where shall we ride?"

"Around the yard."

Ilse stared at the lead line in the captain's hand. "Here? With him?"

The captain called for the stableboy to saddle up the white horse.

"I thought we would go down the mountain," Ilse said. "Please, Father, I wish to ride outside the walls."

"I have duties to which I must attend."

Ilse tossed back her braids. "I do not choose to ride in circles. I have duties to which I must attend." She turned her back on her father and began to walk toward the Ritterhaus.

I sat silently on Tintenfleck, half-dreading, half-eager to see what would happen.

"Ilse!" The voice was a whip crack.

She gave no indication that she had heard.

When Captain von Berlepsch spoke for the second time, his voice was as cold and sharp as a steel blade. "*Fräulein*, you will obey my orders. Come here at once."

Ilse turned to face her father. The very air seemed to crackle between them.

The boy led the white horse out of the stable. Ilse pointedly shifted her gaze to her horse. She chirruped softly, and the white horse pulled loose from the boy and trotted, reins trailing, across the yard. Ilse stroked Eisblume's muzzle and murmured praise, never looking at her father.

At the mounting block Ilse climbed into the saddle with the swift grace I remembered from my first morning in the castle. Then she spoke to the air. "How many circles will be required?"

The captain's face was red, but his voice was calm. "Show young Burkhardt what it means to sit a horse."

Ilse's riding was as dazzling as ever. She and Eisblume moved together so skillfully that my eyes were too slow to catch her signals. At times it seemed as if the horse were the one deciding to speed up or turn while the rider merely anticipated the change.

"How does she do it?" I ventured to ask.

The captain chuckled, and I was relieved to find his good humor restored. "Eisblume's mouth has never been ruined by rough hands at the bit. A touch of the reins against her neck and she turns as smoothly as a lady on a dance floor." I could hear the pride in his voice. "Watch this." He held up a hand to Ilse, and the white horse slowed to a walk.

"Drop the reins," said the captain. Ilse looped the reins to keep them from trailing. Captain von Berlepsch told her to cross her arms, as I had done. Only by a roll of the eyes did Ilse protest.

Once more I watched horse and rider turn figure eights at a walk and a trot and a gallop.

"That mare has never been kicked by a clumsy pair of boots. A subtle pressure, a shifting of weight to one side or the other, and she changes speed or direction."

I patted Tintenfleck's neck, wondering how badly I had abused him during the journey to the Wartburg.

"Your horse has bad habits because you have bad habits," said the captain. "You must unlearn them together." He called across the yard, "Thank you, my dear. You have turned enough circles."

Ilse rode over to the mounting block and slipped down from Eisblume. The stableboy was waiting, but she ignored his outstretched hand and led the mare into the stable herself.

"As in swordsmanship, so in horsemanship," said Captain von Berlepsch. "Balance is all. I do not mean the mere fact of keeping one's seat." He smiled. "I refer to the balance between rider and mount. Because a master expects to be obeyed, a successful master never makes unreasonable demands."

CHAPTER 7

The Place of a Page

One morning Sir Georg handed me his pen-knife and asked me to cut the nibs for some new quills. The little wooden-handled knife seemed a strangely humble tool for a knight. As I turned the knife over and over in my hand, Sir Georg said, "My father gave me that when I first went away to school. I was gifted in learning, and he saw to it that I was educated well. He hoped that I might take up the field of—" The knight stopped abruptly.

After a moment he stroked his beard as if recollecting himself. "*Ach*, it matters not. My father did not understand that I have always been more interested in the Kingdom of the Spirit than the Kingdom of the Sword."

Sir Georg asked me to wait while he finished his writing task, so I sat on my stool listening to the calling birds in the forest below. At last the knight set aside his pen, folded the page, and wrote two lines on the outside. He set the folded paper next to the covered dish on my tray. "Tell the captain this must be sent immediately." Then he laid out a new sheet of paper and picked up his quill again.

Why was a prisoner giving orders to his jailer? The ways of the nobility were strange indeed. In the passageway I tilted my head to read the lines on the packet. A name and a city—Wittenberg. Then I carried my tray down the stairs and called for Otto to open the door.

I found the captain in the gateroom.

"Excuse me, sir," I said. "Sir Georg asked that you send this at once."

Captain von Berlepsch set the folded letter on the table before him. Taking a sheet of heavy paper from beside his maps, he copied the two lines and then folded his own page around Sir Georg's letter. I watched him drip wax onto the paper and press his seal into the wax. Then he handed the letter to Otto and told him to have one of the soldiers carry it down the mountain to Eisenach.

Why did the captain allow a prisoner to correspond with the outside world? What if the knight's allies banded together to rescue their comrade?

"Sir," I ventured, "what if Sir Georg's friends come in search of him?"

"I assure you that none of his friends has the slightest idea where he is hidden."

I wondered whether the knight's letter would actually reach its intended destination.

The captain seemed to read my thoughts. "Sir Georg and I are both men of honor."

"Then why must he be locked in his room?" Belatedly I added "sir" as the captain's steely gaze met mine.

"You forget your place, young Burkhardt. I am the master here, and you are an ignorant child. Get out of my sight."

The captain's words ringing in my ears, I left the Ritterhaus and crossed the courtyard to the pear tree. Leaning back against the trunk, I peered into the branches to see whether Dolf was up there among the nubs of fruit. I was alone. I closed my eyes to shut out the sight of the Wartburg castle grounds. Beyond the nickering of the stabled horses and the squawking of geese, I heard the high clear notes of a pipe or a flute.

Opening my eyes, I began to walk slowly across the yard, drawn toward the sound of the music. I stopped outside the kitchen door, which was propped open. Inside, several trussed fowl and a pile of scallions lay on the chopping block. Steam wafted from the cauldron on the hearth. On the far side of the room dim shafts of sunlight struggled through a soot-darkened window.

On a long bench under the window sat two figures, the smaller one dwarfed by the larger. As Dolf ended the tune and lowered his pipe, the cook's enormous bosom heaved in a sigh. "*Ach*, how your playing takes me back," Gunda said.

Then she saw me in the doorway, and her expression changed to a glower. "What are you staring at?"

"I—I heard the music."

Gunda scowled. "Go back to your own kind. You need not listen to a kitchen boy."

Cheeks burning, I stumbled down the path to the stable, where I wrapped my arms around Tintenfleck's neck and buried my face in his black mane.

"Will I never be rid of you?" Ilse glared at me from beside Eisblume.

I said the first thing that came into my mind. "Why do you dislike me so?"

Her eyes narrowed. "I dislike pretenders."

I wanted to tell her that I disliked pretenders as much as she did. I wanted to say that I had no choice but to follow the captain's orders, just as she did. Instead, I lowered my head and slunk out of the stable past the old gardener stooping among the herbs and the little goose girl with her flock. It seemed I was the only one who did not understand his place at the Wartburg.

At the appointed time for Sir Georg's evening meal, I had to force my feet along the path to the kitchen. Gunda had her back to me, and Dolf was squatting at the hearth, turning the spit as several geese roasted over the fire. I slipped into the room and approached the fireplace. The kitchen boy looked up and then dropped his gaze.

I knelt so I could look into his face. "I have been very rude, and I beg your pardon."

Dolf's blue eyes met mine, and then he turned toward the fire. I remained kneeling beside him, watching the roasting birds turn round and round as the juices dripped and sizzled. Then Dolf pushed back his hair with a greasy hand. "Will you tell me about the prisoner?"

I nodded, and he ventured a crooked little smile.

When I carried the tray to the Ritterhaus, Otto did not meet me with a tankard. At the doorway of the gateroom I stopped in surprise. There at the long table sat Sir Georg and Captain von Berlepsch, each with a tankard before him.

"Don't stand there gawking," said the captain. "Your duty is to serve your lord."

CHAPTER 8

The Tale of the Outlaw

Master Klüglein squawked and flapped his green wings when I entered the gateroom and set the tray before Sir Georg.

"Otto," said Captain von Berlepsch, "bring a drink for young Burkhardt." The soldier bowed and left the room. I could hear his tread on the stairs as I stood waiting for the captain to give some word of command.

Sir Georg said, "Will you break bread with us, Captain? Your cook sends enough for three."

The captain shook his head. "I shall dine with my family. Do not let me keep you from your meal."

"Sit down, Seppel," said the knight. Then he bowed his head to ask the blessing. Before I closed my eyes, I saw the captain watching me.

After the prayer Otto set a tankard before me, then left the room, closing the door behind him.

The captain sipped from his tankard. "There is much rejoicing in Wittenberg. Luther has sent word that he is alive and well."

Sir Georg leaned forward, knife in hand. "And where do they say he is?"

The captain shrugged. "Many assume he is hidden in a monastery, perhaps in Bohemia."

"Hidden in Bohemia!" The knight's voice was bitter. "Then he is a coward indeed. Who but a coward would desert his people in their time of need?"

Captain von Berlepsch set down his tankard and placed his hands on the table, fingers barely touching the wood. "This Thuringian commoner has stood firm against the pope and the emperor and all the forces of Christendom. I will not have him branded a coward. Do I make myself clear?"

To my surprise, Sir Georg smiled. "Is that a threat, Captain? If I were to denounce the notorious Martin Luther, would you banish me from the Wartburg?"

The captain reached for his tankard and raised it high. "To *Herr Doktor* Luther. Long may he fight the good fight."

The knight raised his own tankard, but he did not drink. "If this man is so brave, why does he not return as boldly to Wittenberg as he went forth to Worms?"

I tried to remember what I had heard about the meeting of the emperor and the German princes in the city of Worms. I knew that Luther had been called to account for writing against certain teachings of the church. The Wittenberg professor had been excommunicated by the pope, but according to the villagers in Spalt, Luther was a hero for all of Germany.

"The man is not without enemies," the captain said. "According to the law of church and state, it is the duty of every good Christian to seize Luther and bring him before the authorities for punishment."

"He is well loved in Wittenberg," said the knight, "most especially by the authorities."

"But his return would place his friends in grave danger. Do you not understand, Georg, that those who harbor an outlaw risk being outlawed themselves?"

The captain rummaged through the maps on the table and held up a document. "The proclamation of our new emperor after the Diet of Worms." He pushed the paper to me. "Read it aloud. Begin here."

I cleared my throat and read: "We now command each of you not to lodge or shelter him; not to offer food and drink to him; neither by words nor deeds to offer him any help or assistance—"

"Enough," said Captain von Berlepsch. "Is the meal to your liking, my dear guest?"

"As always, my good host."

The captain pointed to another section of the document. "Begin there."

Again I read aloud: "As for his supporters and followers, you are to overcome and capture them, take hold of their possessions, and use them for your own purposes."

"Enough," said the captain. "I am a soldier, and I see with a soldier's eye. Luther has pressed hard and long against his enemies. Now he steps back to take the measure of their strength. The good doctor is employing a sound military strategy."

Sir Georg snorted. "He is a simple peasant. What does the man know of the knightly arts?"

"A peasant perhaps, but hardly simple." The captain waved a hand over the table. "Your food grows cold. Eat, my noble friend, while I tell young Burkhardt the tale of this notorious outlaw."

Captain von Berlepsch rolled up the imperial proclamation and tossed it carelessly aside. "Four years ago Martin Luther posted a set of theses, public statements in which he objected to the selling of pardons by the pope. These indulgences, as they are called, are—"

"—a knavish trick," Sir Georg cut in, "designed to swindle the ignorant and fatten the purses of Rome." He turned to me. "I ask you, Seppel, can the grace of God be bought and sold like a pair of boots or a loaf of bread? Yet Rome would have us believe that the purchase of a piece of paper actually grants the buyer forgiveness of sins. Pay your money and redeem yourself from many years in purgatory, cry the indulgence sellers in the market square."

The knight picked up a rolled document from the table. "You there in the crowd, are you not a loyal son? Will you not offer part of your inheritance to release your dear father from purgatory? Remember this, my friends—When money in the coffer rings, another soul to heaven springs!"

Captain von Berlepsch unfurled a map. "Such are the wonders of our age that the printed word can travel as swiftly as a man on horseback. In a matter of weeks all of Germany had seen copies of Luther's theses. Peasants and princes, merchants and students murmured that Luther was right, that the wealth of the Roman Church had been gained by deceiving the German people."

Sir Georg leaned forward. "Naturally, those who grow rich on the pious offerings of dutiful Christians do not care to have their crimes exposed."

"Luther was accused of spreading false doctrine," said the captain. "Pope Leo summoned him to Rome to answer to charges of heresy."

He grimaced. "The accused who go to Rome on such charges seldom return. However, wise Duke Frederick was keeping watch over his famous professor, thanks to Spalatin, an old colleague of Luther."

I tried to hide my surprise at the mention of my uncle's name.

Pointing to the map, the captain said, "First in Augsburg and later in Leipzig, Luther was called upon to defend his writings."

"Which he did quite ably," said Sir Georg, "on the basis of *sola Scriptura*, the Bible alone."

"But even as Luther's words were winning the hearts of the German people," said Captain von Berlepsch, "the powers of church and state were closing in. Old Emperor Maximilian died, and when the seven electors cast their votes for a new emperor, they chose Duke Frederick, who declined the title. On the second ballot they elected Maximilian's grandson, Charles. Pope Leo demanded that Charles uphold the excommunication of the German heretic. Thus it was that Luther was summoned to appear before the new emperor at the Diet of Worms. Many feared that even the support of Duke Frederick would not save Luther from an untimely death."

The captain turned again to the map. "An imperial herald led the way as Luther and his companions rode in a borrowed wagon from Wittenberg to Worms." The captain's finger traced the route. "In every village and town Luther was cheered—"

"—or jeered," said Sir Georg. "There were many who cursed him for treason against the church."

Captain von Berlepsch nodded. "True. In Erfurt and Frankfort, crowds gathered to see the man whose name was known in every household. As the travelers approached Worms, a hundred knights galloped out of the gates to escort Luther into the city. Thousands of people lined the streets to wish him well." The captain chuckled. "This was hardly the reception that the pope and the emperor had intended for the German heretic."

Pushing aside the map, the captain took another drink from his tankard. "The next day Luther stood in the presence of the emperor, the German princes, and the pope's representative from Rome. An assortment of Luther's books was laid out on a table. The good doctor was asked just two questions. First, did he acknowledge that he had written these works? Second, was he prepared to defend their content or would he now recant them?"

Sir Georg pushed aside his platter.

"The books were named to him one by one," said the captain, "and Luther admitted that these were indeed his works. As for the question of recanting, he asked to be allowed time to think the matter over. He was ordered to return the next day with his answer."

The captain glanced at the knight before he turned back to me. "On that afternoon Luther stood once more before the Diet. First in Latin and then in German, the question was put to him again. Did he wish to defend his books or to recant?"

Sir Georg said, "First in Latin and then in German, Luther tried to explain the nature of his writings. He asked the assembly to use evidence from Holy Scripture to overthrow his teaching. 'Once I have been taught,' he said, 'I shall be quite ready to renounce every error, and I shall be the first to cast my books into the fire.'"

The captain leaned forward. "Luther was told that all that was required was a simple response. Did he or did he not choose to recant?"

Again Sir Georg took up the tale. "'I cannot and I will not retract anything,' Luther told the assembly, 'since it is neither safe nor right to go against conscience. I cannot do otherwise. Here I stand, may God help me.'"

The silence that fell over the room was broken at last by the squawking of the parrot.

The captain drained his tankard. "They say that when Luther left the hall, he raised his arms above his head like a champion." He began to roll up the map. "My noble guest, you have the freedom of the castle grounds. Tomorrow I shall send my daughter to accompany you on a tour of the Wartburg."

CHAPTER 9

Freedom of the Grounds

The next morning I wondered where I would find Sir Georg. I was surprised to see him seated at the table, quill in hand. Why was he not savoring his new freedom? Apart from last night's visit to the gateroom, the knight had not set foot outside of his chamber since I had arrived at the castle.

I sat on the stool with the tray on my knees and waited for Sir Georg to put down his quill. After we finished our meal and returned thanks to God, the knight said, "Now, Seppel, what an adventure we shall have. I am eager to see more of the Wartburg."

"Should you take your sword, sir?"

The captain was never without a sidearm, which seemed as much a part of him as his beard. I had never seen Sir Georg wearing his sword, and I had given up trying to figure out why a prisoner was allowed to have a weapon. As I often told myself, the ways of the nobility were strange indeed.

"I suppose I should." The knight looked around the room. "Have you seen it?"

I lifted the sword from the stack of papers in a corner. "Here it is, sir."

Sir Georg fumbled in buckling the sword belt. Glancing up as if to see whether I had noticed, he said, "I am certainly out of practice."

At last we left the chamber and descended the narrow stairwell. Otto no longer guarded the door, and no one was in the gateroom except Master Klüglein, who rasped a greeting from his perch. The knight and I descended the stairs and stepped out into the courtyard.

Sir Georg blinked in the bright morning light. Under the curly black beard his skin was very pale. How difficult this confinement must be for a man used to the hardy life of a knight. Sir Georg crossed the yard and stood underneath the pear tree, his face shaded by the leaves. He reached out his hand and touched one of the tiny knobs of fruit.

"Under just such a tree as this, I was called to—" He stopped abruptly, then spoke the phrase I heard so often. "*Ach*, it matters not."

At a rustling in the leaves, we both looked up to see Dolf peering down, his blue eyes wide.

Sir Georg smiled. "Who is here—a young Zaccheus? Come down, come down."

With a creak of branches the kitchen boy dropped to the ground and stared up at the knight. "I'm not called Zaccheus, sir."

"Of course not," said Sir Georg. "You are Dolf, and I am very pleased to meet you."

Dolf grinned at me. "You're right. He's not horrible at all."

The knight's laugh echoed across the courtyard. "There are some who would disagree." He placed one hand on my shoulder and the other on Dolf's. "Show me to the kitchen that I might meet the incomparable Gunda."

As we approached the kitchen, the knight told us a story of a little man who climbed a tree to see a great teacher, Jesus of Nazareth. "Just as Jesus invited himself into the home of Zaccheus, so he invites himself into our homes and hearts. Our Lord is both host and guest. When we welcome him, we share the feast that only he can provide."

In the kitchen Gunda's arms were white to the elbow as she pummeled an enormous batch of dough. Sir Georg strode boldly into the room while Dolf and I lingered in the doorway.

Gunda punched the dough again with one enormous fist. "If you have no business in my kitchen, then be gone. I have work to do."

Sir Georg seemed to take no offense. He bowed. "I thank you for your many services to me."

The cook stared at him, hands still buried in the dough.

The knight smiled. "Did not our Lord teach us to ask for our daily bread? Do you not provide all of us in the castle with that which sustains our bodies?"

The cook's floury brow was furrowed, her mouth open in suspicion.

"Good *Frau* Gunda, by the very nature of your calling you are an answer to prayer. *Gott sei dank*—God be thanked for you."

Gunda blinked at him, mumbled something, and returned to kneading the dough.

Sir Georg gazed at the great stone hearth, the soot-blackened cauldron, the rafters hung with iron pots and pans and all the implements of the cook's trade. Then he made his way to the window and picked up Dolf's pipe from the sill. "Who is the musician?"

"I am, sir."

"Play a tune for me, if you please. I have gone too long without music."

Dolf took the pipe and looked at Gunda, who shrugged and continued to knead the dough. Sir Georg sat down on the bench under the window and beckoned me to sit beside him.

Dolf held the pipe uncertainly. "What would you like me to play, sir?"

"Do you know this one?" Sir Georg began to hum. After a few tentative notes the pipe joined in as the knight sang clear and true:

> The country and the people with whom my life passed by
> From childhood are estranged as if 'twere all a lie.
> They who were once my playmates have weary grown and old.
> The meadows have been broken—the woods cut down and sold.

The knight sang of laughter turned to weeping, of a beautiful world turned dark and dead. I saw Gunda swipe at her eyes with a floury hand. The words carried me back to Spalt. Even now my sisters might be out picking strawberries for Mother, coming home with full baskets and crimson-stained mouths. But someday they would all be gone, along with the fields and forests where we used to romp. When would I see them again? My throat grew tight, and I ducked my head so none of them could see my eyes.

In the last verse Sir Georg sang of a mighty prize that was neither lands nor gold.

> But, oh, a wondrous crown for evermore to wear,
> Which e'en the poorest soldier may win him with his spear.
> Yea, if that crusade noble I might follow o'er the sea,
> I evermore should sing "All's well!" and nevermore "Ah, me!"

Dolf finished the song with a flourish and cradled his pipe. "Walther von der Vogelweide was the greatest of the old singers," he said, adding proudly, "He lived here at the Wartburg."

Sir Georg nodded. "The man's poetry is masterful, but I must question his theology. Neither the poorest soldier nor the greatest can ever win that heavenly crown."

The knight made a gesture of emptiness, hands apart. "No crusade, no pilgrimage, no gold or lands, no act of a man can ever make him worthy of God's forgiveness. The law of God tells us that we are all sinners. We all fall short."

Except for the crackling of the fire, the room was silent. Even Gunda stood absolutely still. Achingly I thought of my father in purgatory. I touched the pouch under my tunic. Why had I not yet found a priest to say that Mass?

"What the poet does not sing," said Sir Georg softly, "is the Gospel." He cupped his hands together. "The grace of God is given to us in full measure. Forgiveness cannot be purchased or earned. The gift is ours through faith alone."

A dark silhouette blocked the bright doorway, and a terse voice rang through the room. "Georg, I must speak to you at once."

The knight bowed again to the cook before he left the kitchen. Not wishing to remain near Gunda without the mellowing influence of music, I began to sidle quietly toward the door. Then I halted, hearing the angry whisper of Captain von Berlepsch.

"*Bei allen Heilingen!* Have you lost your senses? You cannot converse with servants as though you were the village priest."

"How can I do otherwise, Captain?" Sir Georg sounded amused.

"I do not wish to discuss the matter. You are to refrain from all actions unbecoming a knight. Do I make myself clear?"

"My dear host, I am greatly in your debt. However, neither the pope nor the emperor has yet been able to silence me. It seems unlikely that you can do what the devil cannot."

For a long moment I heard nothing more.

At last the captain spoke. "*Herr Doktor*, you must understand that your safety is my gravest concern. Your life has been placed in my hands. I will do all within my power to preserve it. I would appreciate your cooperation."

I leaned against the kitchen wall, hardly able to comprehend the astounding truth about the man I knew as Sir Georg.

CHAPTER 10

View from the Mountain

As I wondered whether I had heard the captain correctly, I heard quick footsteps in the yard. I inched over to the doorway to glimpse the flash of red hair in the sun. Ilse stopped before the monk in knight's clothing, the outlawed professor Martin Luther himself.

"Good morning, Sir Georg," she said. "I am most pleased to meet you."

"Have I taught you nothing?" said Captain von Berlepsch. "It is not fitting to address a man so boldly."

"But Sir Georg is our guest. You said so yourself."

I leaned out to see how the captain would respond. "Has the world turned upside-down? Knights who preach to the servants. Daughters who contradict their fathers—" Suddenly his eye caught mine. Too late I drew back from the door. "And pages who spy on their lords." Each word was as punishing as a blow.

I stepped out into the yard. Even with my head bowed, I could feel Ilse's scornful gaze on me.

"How long have you been skulking about?" said the captain.

"I heard the voice of *Fräulein* Ilse. You said she was to show Sir Georg the castle grounds."

"I know what I said. Look at me, young Burkhardt."

I tried to meet his eyes, but I could not read what I saw there.

Beside the captain, Sir Georg's face was a mask.

"Fetch the keys to the palace," said the captain. "You will find them behind Master Klüglein's perch."

I hurried across the yard, wishing that the pounding in my ears would block out the questions in my head. Did the captain realize that I had overheard him? Who else at the Wartburg knew the knight's true identity?

Charging up the stairs of the Ritterhaus two at a time, I arrived breathlessly at the gateroom. As I reached behind the perch for the iron ring of keys, I wondered what the captain would do if he found out what I knew. Would he turn me out of the castle? Would he keep me in a locked room?

The green parrot's curved beak moved fast. I yelped and stared at the gash on my hand.

"Was sehrt, das lehrt!" said the obnoxious bird.

Clutching my sore hand, I was tempted to ask Otto to get the keys. However, I did not want to be mastered by a bird called Mister Know-It-All. I studied my opponent's hard little eyes and wrinkled claws.

Master Klüglein watched me curiously as I stooped to grasp the iron base and drag the heavy perch away from the wall, metal scraping over slate. Then I held my hand temptingly close to the staring round eyes. When the curved beak shot forward, I ducked under the perch and snatched the ring of keys.

I trotted back across the courtyard in time to hear Ilse say, "I'm sure Sir Georg would rather ride in the forest than walk around in empty rooms."

"You will refrain from impertinence or return to your needlework."

Ilse's eyes narrowed dangerously at my approach.

Captain von Berlepsch said to the knight, "My wife requests your presence in the Ritterhaus when you have finished your tour." He strode off across the courtyard.

"Page," said Ilse, "you are to follow with the keys." She slipped her hand into the crook of Sir Georg's elbow.

The knight started, then caught himself.

Clearly, Ilse did not know the knight's real identity, for she would never have behaved so cozily with a monk. I felt a selfish glee. Ilse despised my pretense, but she was in the company of a greater pretender than I. She might think me ignorant, but I knew the secret of the Wartburg. I clanked the keys cheerfully as we entered the inner courtyard.

Ilse looked back in annoyance, but Sir Georg smiled. I wondered whether he would treat me as warmly if he knew what power I held. The very thought made me giddy. I remembered the document I had read aloud in the gateroom. If outlaws were to be offered neither food nor shelter, then I violated the emperor's decree every time I carried a tray to Sir Georg's room.

As we stood beside the cistern, Ilse said to the knight, "Dame Adela has asked me to tell you the history of the Wartburg." She sounded as if she hoped he would suggest a different topic.

While Ilse rattled off a long list of the rulers of Thuringia, I studied Sir Georg. How had I ever mistaken him for a knight? He was nothing like Sir Gottfried or other armed horsemen I had seen back in Spalt. Had Doctor Luther been schooled in swordsmanship and horsemanship as I had? Captain von Berlepsch was indeed the Lord of Parrots. How skillfully he had taught us commoners to mimic the ways of the nobility!

I followed my companions up the stone steps of the palace. Ilse pointed to a stone carving over the door. An ancient warrior was locked in struggle with a winged beast. "There is your namesake, Sir Georg."

"If only my dragons were so easily vanquished."

At Ilse's command I unlocked the door and pulled it open, wondering whether the captain or the outlaw himself had chosen the name of the dragon-slayer.

When I closed the door, the three of us stood in the cool dim world of an age long past. Sunlight slanted through double-arched windows. The walls glowed with intricate patterns of scarlet and gold and blue. An adjoining room was clearly a banqueting-hall. On a raised platform stood a long table and chairs. At the far end of the room, a row of columns framed a narrow stage.

Ilse said, "This is the Singers' Hall."

"The site of the *Sängerkrieg*!" Sir Georg turned to me. "Seppel, in this very room the greatest of musicians gathered for the Tournament of Song." He stepped onto the stage. "*Fräulein* Ilse, surely you agree that music is one of God's finest gifts."

"I would gladly trade my lute for a gallop down the Singers' Way."

Sir Georg's laughter echoed in the room. "Seppel has told me what a fine horsewoman you are."

Ilse did not seem pleased to learn that I had been speaking of her.

She led us out onto a roofed arcade that ran along the second floor of the palace. "Here is where the Landgravine Elisabeth fainted when she heard her husband had been killed on a crusade. Afterward she pined away like the turtledove in the old saying."

Sir Georg shook his head. "I do not know that saying."

Ilse chanted, "The good woman who is widowed, like a turtledove is she. She mourns for her mate on a withered twig and lets the green one be."

Then she frowned. "And do you know what the 'good man' does when he is widowed?"

Again Sir Georg shook his head.

"He takes a new wife that he might get himself a son." Ilse glared at me, then turned and disappeared into the palace.

Sir Georg looked at me in bewilderment. "I confess I know very little about women. I am not at all eager to have a wife thrust upon me."

I stifled a laugh at the idea of a monk taking a wife. I wanted desperately to tell him what I knew.

"Seppel, you know *Fräulein* Ilse better than I do. Are we expected to search for her?"

"Perhaps she doesn't want to be found."

"Then let us continue our tour alone."

The knight and I climbed another staircase to a gallery that opened onto a festival hall occupying the entire third floor. As I admired the fancifully carved birds and beasts that adorned the columns supporting the roof, I saw a figure silhouetted in a high window. Ilse might have been a bird perched lightly on a sill. I could not understand how she had managed to get up there without flying.

Sir Georg's voice rang out over the hall: "*Fräulein* Ilse, what a delightful view you must have. May we come up to join you?"

The knight and I crossed the long room to a little door that led to a winding stair. At the top of the staircase, we stepped out onto a balcony. The countryside was spread out below me like the captain's map. The faraway cluster of red rooftops must be the town of Eisenach.

Sir Georg said, "'The Lord is my strength, my fortress, and my high tower.' With the psalmist I rejoice: 'Yea, thou liftest me up above those who rise up against me.'" He turned to Ilse. "And do you rejoice in this view from the mountain?"

Ilse shrugged. "Why should a prisoner rejoice? We must return to the Ritterhaus. My mother and Dame Adela are expecting you."

As we crossed the courtyard to the Ritterhaus, I wondered whether Lady von Berlepsch and Dame Adela knew Sir Georg's true identity. Would the captain confide in his wife or would he keep such dangerous knowledge from his household? Again I grew almost giddy at the thought that I knew something that others did not.

In the ladies' chamber Sir Georg bowed precisely as I had done on my first venture into this room. Dame Adela directed him to a chair near the couch where Lady von Berlepsch reclined. Ilse seated herself next to the chess table.

I stood at the door, apparently forgotten.

Dame Adela said, "I hope you enjoyed your tour of the palace. It is most unfortunate that my family no longer dwells within those walls. I am a descendant of Saint Elisabeth herself."

"I am deeply honored to meet you, dear lady." The knight's tone was solemn, but I detected secret amusement.

Ilse waved a hand over the chessboard. "Sir Georg, would you care to play?"

I wondered whether monks or professors played chess. If not, how would the disguised outlaw respond?

Sir Georg touched one of the carved figures, then another. As if to himself he said, "Yes, kingdoms and empires come and go, and they are our Lord God's chess game."

Ilse's brow wrinkled in bewilderment. I almost laughed aloud.

Sir Georg turned to Lady von Berlepsch. "You and the captain are most gracious hosts. The view from the mountain has made me eager to experience the beauty of the Thuringian Forest. Would you ask your husband whether I might ride outside the walls? Perhaps your daughter could accompany me. She was a most charming companion on our tour of the palace."

A long silence hung over the room. Lady von Berlepsch seemed completely taken aback. Even Dame Adela had nothing to say. I studied the two women's faces, trying to figure out whether they knew that their house guest was the most famous outlaw in Germany.

Ilse's eyes darted from the knight to her mother and back again. "Please, Mother. Ask Father to let us ride."

At last Lady von Berlepsch sighed. "I will speak to the captain," she said.

CHAPTER 11

The Tale of the Drover

During a long stretch of torrid summer days, Lady von Berlepsch kept to her chamber. I did not know whether she had spoken to the captain about allowing the knight to venture outside the walls. In any case, Sir Georg was in no condition to ride. He suffered from stomach ailments and a most distressing bowel condition. When he was not pacing his room like a chained animal, he was lying on his bed, drenched in sweat and doubled over in pain.

One morning he waved the tray away. "Tell the captain I must go to the doctors in Erfurt. This cannot continue. I must have some relief."

Captain von Berlepsch was in the courtyard with Otto. Wearing padded leather caps, the two men circled each other like menacing dogs. Each gripped a long staff in both hands. The first move came so fast my eye could barely follow the feint, thrust, and crack of the wood.

Hermina stood beside me, clutching her apron. She gasped when Otto took a hit. When his next blow sent the captain staggering, she fairly bounced with glee.

The captain cursed, then called out, "On your guard, man. You will not touch me again."

With his forearm Otto pushed damp hair from his face. "As you wish, sir."

Again the circling, the sudden thrust, and then a flurry of blows. This time the thwack of the captain's staff against the side of Otto's head made Hermina shriek. Panting, the two men threw down their staves, tossed aside their leather helmets, and embraced heartily.

Hermina hurried toward Otto, exclaiming over the blood trickling down his cheek.

The captain waved her away. "It is a scratch, nothing more. If you wish to do well by your man, bring him a dipper of water. Bring me another."

He turned to me, wiping sweat from his forehead. "What do you want?"

When I reported what Sir Georg had said, the captain cursed again. "Ailments, always these mysterious ailments. Give me a real opponent. How can one fight against a disease?"

To Otto he said, "I will go to Erfurt myself."

Within the hour Captain von Berlepsch rode out of the Wartburg.

Sir Georg wished to be left alone, and I had no lessons with the captain and no appointment with the noblewomen. I felt quite idle and sluggish in the heat.

I heard the voices of Otto and Hermina in the front hall of the Ritterhaus. When she saw me, Hermina said, "Can you believe it, Seppel? Dame Adela has ordered us to move the household into the palace. She claims the change in air will improve the health of Lady von Berlepsch."

Otto shrugged. "It's true that the stone walls keep the palace cool."

Hermina made an exasperated noise. "It's no accident that she waited until the captain left the castle!"

"Keep your temper, dear one. The day is hot enough."

In the sweltering heat, the castle servants loaded carts with bundles and chairs and chests and trundled them across the courtyard and up the stone steps of the palace. Later Otto and three other men carried Lady von Berlepsch in a covered litter to her new rooms. I suspect Dame Adela would have liked to be carried in a litter as well, but she and Ilse walked alongside instead.

I spent the evening with Otto and Hermina in the servants' quarters on the ground floor of the palace. We sat on benches that ran the length of rough unpainted walls. Thick unadorned columns supported the brilliantly decorated rooms above us. Hermina sat with her mending, just as Mother used to do.

Even now Mother and my sisters might be sitting in the cottage with their needlework. I remembered when little Annchen mended a tear in Father's cloak. Her long crooked stitches made Renata and Ludmilla laugh. Annchen cried, but Father wore that cloak proudly and did not allow anyone to change a single stitch.

My throat tight, I said to Hermina, "The captain went to seek help for Sir Georg. Why doesn't he get a doctor for his own wife?"

"Doctors have come and gone. They say her life is now in the hand of God." Hermina sighed. "Many a good lady has met an ill fate at the Wartburg. Not only blessed Saint Elisabeth, but also the poor Landgravine Margaret. Otto, you must tell Seppel that story."

Otto shifted his weight on the bench. "Long, long ago," he said, his voice slow and rhythmic, "Thuringia was ruled by the Landgrave Albrecht and his good wife Margaret. One night at a banquet in the palace, the Landgrave was smitten by the beauty of the Lady Kunigunde."

Hermina giggled. "That is our Gunda's true name."

Otto nodded. "The Kunigunde of the story was perhaps not so fine a cook, but she had other charms. Night and day Albrecht thought only of Kunigunde. At last he determined to make her his own. But the Lady Kunigunde would have none of him. 'What am I to you?' she said. 'You already have a wife and sons.' But while her words told him one thing, her eyes promised another."

Otto leaned forward. "There was a servant of the castle whose duty it was to drive the donkey trains up the mountain. In secret, Albrecht ordered the drover to slip into Margaret's chamber and strangle her in her bed."

I straightened up. "But why would the drover agree to do that?"

Hermina said, "He must have been a great sinner already. It might be that he was a thief or a drunkard."

"That is not part of the story," said Otto. "The story is that the drover did indeed creep into the lady's chamber, but when Margaret awoke in fright, he threw himself on his knees before her. 'Good lady, I would rather die than kill you,' he whispered in great remorse. 'If you know some way, you might save both yourself and me.'"

Hermina clicked her tongue. "That's not true remorse. The drover just wanted to save himself."

Otto frowned. "The point is that he did not commit this terrible crime."

"But he would have done so, Otto, if he believed he would not be caught."

"Bei allen Heiligen!" said Otto, sounding very much like the captain. "I can tell the story only as it was told to me." He cleared his throat. "The Landgravine summoned her steward, whom she trusted above anyone else in the household. The drover confessed all, and when the steward heard that the lady's husband himself was behind the plan, he said, 'My lady, your life will never be safe within these walls. You must flee at once.'"

"Now listen, Seppel," said Hermina. "Here comes the saddest part."

Otto said, "Good Margaret could not bear to leave without saying farewell to her children. She wept and kissed them, and in her grief she bit the cheek of her older son. He carried the mark all his life."

Hermina nodded. "For all his life, he was known as Frederick with the Bite."

"Then the steward and the drover and the lady and one of her maids crept secretly from the palace to the Ritterhaus. From a window in the drover's room, the steward lowered the other three in a huge basket."

Remembering the height of the castle walls, I shivered as I imagined the three clutching the rope as the basket sank lower and lower in the darkness.

"Good Margaret found refuge in Frankfurt," said Otto, "but she died of grief within the year."

Hermina wrinkled her brow. "I wonder what became of the drover."

"Dear one, this is the story of the Landgravine Margaret. What does it matter what became of a servant?"

Hermina turned to me. "Seppel, don't you agree that the good people in stories are hardly ever as interesting as the wicked ones?"

I had never thought of that. "It's true. Good people are often very dull."

Otto threw up his hands. "Then may God grant us all an exceedingly dull life."

CHAPTER 12

Outside the Walls

Two days later Captain von Berlepsch returned to the Wartburg. The doctor in Erfurt prescribed medication, a change in diet, and more physical activity for Sir Georg. The knight brightened at hearing the doctor's name. "He was an old classmate of mine at the university."

The captain raised an eyebrow. "Georg, please remember to think before you speak."

The two men were seated in the gateroom while Otto and I stood watch by the door.

The medicine had a cheering effect on the knight, but the captain was somber indeed.

According to Hermina, Captain von Berlepsch had been most displeased to find his household established in the palace: "And then the captain told them he did not care whether Dame Adela was the descendant of Saint Elisabeth or the Blessed Virgin herself! He said that the guardian of the Wartburg belonged in the Ritterhaus, not the palace. Did his women think they were princesses or landgravines themselves? He said they could pretend they were Thuringian royalty as long as they wanted, but he himself was going to dine in the knights' quarters with Sir Georg."

While Hermina delighted in reporting the goings-on in the family von Berlepsch, I was sometimes uneasy hearing such accounts. At times the nobility seemed no better than the most quarrelsome families back in Spalt.

The next morning during my lesson in the armory, I circled Captain von Berlepsch, wooden practice sword in hand, trying in vain to find that elusive opening.

The captain laughed. "Are you a swordsman or a dancing master?"

I lunged at him with my ridiculous weapon, but he merely smiled as he parried my furious attack. Our blades locked hilt to hilt, and

I pressed as hard as I could, grunting with exertion. In frustration I pulled back. At the sudden absence of pressure the other blade slid past mine. In that instant I drove my sword home, and the blunt end hit the captain's tunic directly above the heart.

Astonished, I looked into my opponent's face.

The captain grinned. "Not bad, young Burkhardt. One would hardly take you for a peasant." Sheathing his weapon, he crossed the room and returned with another sword, smaller and lighter than his own. He carried the sword in both hands, balancing the hilt and flat of the blade on his open palms. I knew enough to recognize that this old-fashioned sword had been wrought by a skilled artisan.

"This belonged to my father," said the captain, "and to his father before him." He held out the sword. "It is yours to carry in the service of Duke Frederick, Elector of Saxony."

I could think of nothing to say.

"Your most important duty is to protect Sir Georg."

"Yes, sir," I said, wondering what harm could befall the disguised Luther within these walls.

"If it is necessary for you to risk your own life for his, I expect you to do so. Do I make myself clear?"

"Yes, sir."

"You will kneel."

I got to my knees on the hard slate floor. His voice low, the captain said, "Josef Burkhardt, I offer this sword in the name of our risen Lord. May you wield it wisely and well."

At his nod I grasped the hilt in my right hand. The captain took my other hand and helped me to my feet. Then he stepped back as I admired the sword's heft and took a few practice swings.

Captain von Berlepsch cleared his throat. "Now tell Sir Georg to put aside his scribbling and join us for a ride outside the walls."

Sir Georg insisted on adding a few more lines to his work. I watched impatiently as he held the quill poised. At last he pushed back his chair. As we left the chamber, I had to remind him to bring his sword.

In the muddy courtyard the white mare was already trotting in circles. Under a green cap with a curved brim and a jaunty feather, Ilse looked happier than I had ever before seen her. At the stable door a boy stood holding the reins of the captain's horse, a bright bay.

In the stable Tintenfleck whinnied eagerly at my approach. While I saddled him, I saw a groom saddling a stocky chestnut for Sir Georg. I wondered whether the knight's skill in horsemanship was as newly acquired as my own.

In the courtyard Captain von Berlepsch signaled his daughter to dismount and waved away the groom and the stableboy. Sir Georg and Ilse and I led our horses down the passage under the Ritterhaus to the gate. When the soldier on guard swung open the door, I felt a rush of joy at the sight of the world beyond the castle walls.

As Ilse picked up her skirts and led Eisblume through the gate, I glimpsed dark stockings above russet boots. The white mare moved up alongside and then passed the captain's bay.

"Ilse!" The captain's voice was sharp. "You will proceed with more decorum."

Ilse gazed out over the treetops below the rocky outcropping of the mountain. Breathing deeply, she lifted her head like some alert, wild creature. "I smell raspberries," she said, "and fir trees, and the faintest whiff of something unpleasant."

I inhaled, but I could not detect any unpleasant smell. Ilse wrinkled her nose at me and pulled Eisblume ahead so that the white tail swished against my face.

Captain von Berlepsch directed us to lead our horses down the steep path. He called a halt at a level spot where the path forked. "Here we will mount."

As Ilse gathered up her skirts, the captain added, "Young Burkhardt, assist my daughter."

Ilse and I stood nearly face to face, but she did not even look at me as she put one hand on my shoulder and placed a mud-splattered boot into the stirrup of my laced fingers. I felt her weight for just a moment before the green skirts sailed up and over Eisblume's back.

The captain murmured to Sir Georg, "Should we meet any person of rank, I will introduce you. Remember that you are to take no notice of commoners." He swung up into the saddle.

Sir Georg mounted his horse with considerably less grace. I looked to see whether Ilse had noticed the knight's clumsiness, but the white mare was already well ahead of us down the trail.

I had no trouble holding Tintenfleck steady while I mounted. As we trotted after the others, I smiled to think how foolish I must have looked on horseback when I arrived at the Wartburg two months ago. Studying the riders on the trail ahead, I marveled to think that the son of a tanner was traveling in such company.

Captain von Berlepsch, girded with sword and dagger, was a compelling figure in his black tunic and close-fitting soldier's cap. No one could mistake the young woman in green for other than his daughter. The dark-haired knight in scarlet appeared as noble as his companions. I hoped that no one we met would look too closely at the fair-haired page on the little black horse.

During that first outing on the steep forest paths surrounding the Wartburg, we sometimes rode so closely that our horses were almost nose to tail. For long stretches we rode in silence. In the beauty of the great Thuringian Forest, I stopped thinking about differences in age and rank and circumstance. When a turn of the trail left me out of sight of my companions, I felt like part of the rugged landscape itself.

The terrain leveled off slightly, and the path broadened into a long open slope. Captain von Berlespch said to Sir Georg, "Here we enter the Singers' Way, where the minstrels began the rivalry that led to the Tournament of Song."

The knight turned to me. "Can you picture that, Seppel? The greatest musicians of the age, each with his lute slung over his shoulder, climbing toward the high court of Thuringia."

Ilse frowned. "I don't care for those old stories." She gestured toward the valley. "I have a fast horse and a good road. I'll meet you at the Dragon's Gorge."

The captain said, "You will ride with me until I tell you to do otherwise."

Abruptly the white mare wheeled and pulled up in front of the captain's bay, which snorted and plunged to a stop. The two horses stood with muzzles nearly touching, pale and dark nostrils flaring. Sir Georg and I reined in our mounts and watched the captain and his daughter.

Ilse lifted her chin. "Why did you teach me to ride if you won't allow me to do so?"

She and her father glared at one another across their horses' heads. The bay shifted his weight, and the bridle jangled.

The captain gave a curt nod. "Ilse, I order you to ride to the Dragon's Gorge."

It was comical to see her puzzle over those words. Then she scowled at her father, wheeled Eisblume, and galloped away down the mountain.

Captain von Berlepsch turned to Sir Georg. "Raising a daughter takes more effort than any military campaign." He seemed to remember my presence. "What are you waiting for? Ride to meet her at the Dragon's Gorge!"

A moment later I was clinging to the saddle in a very unhorsemanlike manner during the most terrifying ride of my life. Pelting down a mountainside with trees flashing by on either side was vastly different from loping in circles under the captain's watchful eye. At first my senses were overwhelmed by pounding hooves and rushing air and a paralyzing fear triggered by the violent movement of the horse beneath me. Then the sword banging against my thigh served to remind me that balance is all, and I recognized the rocking rhythm of the gallop.

Ahead I could see the white flanks of Eisblume. Ilse was leaning so far forward that she was nearly invisible on the mare's back. Just once I glimpsed her face peering back at me, and I urged Tintenfleck on, flattening myself against the wind-whipped mane. I knew we could never catch them. Even if I were a master horseman, Tintenfleck could never match the flying strides of the white mare. Yet we charged valiantly down the mountain, and I felt a thrill when I gained significantly on Ilse by the time she reached the bottom of the slope.

I reined in Tintenfleck and trotted over to where she stood beside Eisblume in the shadow of a towering cleft rock. Both of our horses were lathered and blowing hard.

Ilse's face was flushed. Shining wisps of hair had escaped from under her cap. Her eyes met mine, and she smiled.

I smiled back.

Instantly her face changed. "We must cool off the horses," she said, sounding like her father.

I dismounted and loosened Tintenfleck's girth strap.

Ilse did not smile again, but as we walked the horses in a wide circle near the great cleft, she told me about the long ravine that snaked through this mountain. At times the pathway between the sheer rock walls was too narrow even for a man on horseback. According to legend, a huge serpent had once lived in the gorge. The townspeople made the dragon slayer their patron saint.

"Everything around Eisenach is named after Georg," Ilse said. "Georg's street, Georg's school, and even Georg's monastery on the other side of the mountain."

I wondered whether that was why the name had been chosen for the outlaw. Hooking the thumb of one hand through my sword belt, I was pleased to think that I had a small part to play in keeping the secret of this hero.

Ilse glanced at me sharply. "Where did you get that sword? Let me see it."

I unsheathed the weapon, and the blade glinted in the sunlight.

"How dare you carry a von Berlepsch sword?"

"The captain gave it to me."

"Liar! You must have stolen it. My father would never give an upstart peasant what is rightfully mine!"

CHAPTER 13

The Dragon's Gorge

None of the captain's lessons in the armory had prepared me for an opponent like Ilse von Berlepsch. I stepped back and slid the sword into its sheath. "I beg your pardon, *Fräulein*," I said, hanging my head the way Dolf did when Gunda was on a rampage.

"I don't know why my father brought you to the Wartburg," Ilse said, "but I will never allow you to take what is mine. Give me that sword." She held out her hand, her manner so commanding that instinctively I moved to obey.

The captain rode into the clearing, followed by Sir Georg.

Ilse pointed an accusing finger. "Father, how dare you give him that sword?"

"And how dare you speak to me that way?" The captain met her furious gaze with an unblinking stare. "I will do as I please with what is mine. I am not interested in discussing the matter. We will return to the castle at once."

Abruptly Ilse took the reins in one hand, gathered her skirts in the other, and swung up onto the white mare. A moment later Eisblume thundered away toward the mountain.

The captain turned his horse. "To the Wartburg."

We rode at a brisk trot, but Captain von Berlepsch made no attempt to catch up with his daughter. None of us spoke again on that first journey outside the walls. When the path up the mountain grew steep, the captain signaled us to dismount and lead the horses up to the drawbridge.

Above the great door I saw Ilse framed in the gateroom window. After the captain raised his hand to acknowledge her, she disappeared from view.

At the stable I took the reins of Sir Georg's horse.

"Thank you, Seppel. I am most eager to return to my work." With a nod to the captain, the knight hurried across the yard to the Ritterhaus.

The captain shook his head. "I do not understand these scribblers." Then he eyed me keenly. "You know, of course, that Sir Georg is more scholarly than other knights. His father was a great patron of the arts."

"Yes, sir."

A few days later the captain took Sir Georg and me riding outside the walls once more. Deep in the forest he halted the horses at a fork in the trail, where we met another horseman, a big-bellied gray-bearded nobleman in hunting gear. "Lord Hund von Wenkheim," said the captain, "I present to you Georg of Wittenberg."

Sir Georg bowed slightly from his horse. "I am honored to meet you, my lord." His face was very solemn, almost as if he were trying not to smile.

The nobleman studied the knight. "The Lord of Parrots has been keeping you too long indoors," he said. "In all other ways he is a perfect host." He turned to the captain. "You must bring your guest on a hunting party. The ladies will be quite charmed by your visiting knight." He wheeled his horse and trotted off into the forest.

The captain stroked his beard. "My good neighbor is right. A man such as yourself ought to spend more time on horseback." He glanced at the sun. "I have business to conduct in Eisenach. You and your page may ride freely here. See that you return to the Wartburg before the shadows grow long."

He moved his horse a few steps closer to Sir Georg's. "You are to remember that commoners are beneath your notice." To me he said, "Remember your duty to your lord."

After Sir Georg and I watched the captain out of sight, the knight smiled. "I feel like a schoolboy with an unexpected holiday."

While the chestnut ambled along, Sir Georg held the reins loosely in one hand and gestured with the other. "Now, Seppel, what if our Lord Jesus had taken no notice of commoners? Why, he delighted in speaking to simple people. 'Consider the lilies,' he said to them, and 'Think of the birds of the air.' He told stories of lost coins and lost sheep, most simple things indeed."

The knight's reins were slack, and he hardly seemed to notice when the chestnut lowered his head to nibble a tuft of grass.

"And on the night of our Savior's birth, to whom did the angels address their good news? Why, to simple shepherds!"

I gripped my own reins firmly and wondered whether Captain von Berlepsch would blame me if a bolting rabbit startled Sir Georg's horse and unseated this careless rider. "Sir, perhaps we should dismount and walk."

Soon I was leading both horses as Sir Georg strode ahead. "Ah, this is the life I remember from my student days. A brisk hike is preferable to parading about on horseback."

I was glad that neither the captain nor his daughter was present to hear such an unknightly remark.

When we arrived at the cleft of the Dragon's Gorge, the knight said cheerfully, "Now we must leave the horses. Tie them up, if you please."

I stared at him in astonishment. "Sir? Leave the horses?"

"The path through the gorge becomes too narrow for a rider."

I stood stupidly holding the reins, certain that Captain von Berlepsch would not approve of this plan.

Sir Georg gestured toward the stream tumbling noisily out of the gorge. "Listen to that singing brook inviting us to explore her banks." His dark eyes were bright, and his cheeks were flushed above the black beard. I was reminded of the day I feared the mysterious prisoner might be mad.

"Perhaps I should stay with the horses, sir."

"As you wish, Seppel. Take the horses around the mountain on the trail past the monastery. I will meet you at the other end of the gorge."

I felt a flicker of panic. What if the outlawed monk was plotting an escape through the Dragon's Gorge? What if friends—or enemies— awaited him on the other side of the mountain?

"Sir Georg, wait!" I called, hastily looping the horses' reins around a tree branch. "We will go together." I tried to shrug off my fears of what might happen to the horses in our absence. Surely at worst we would have a long walk back to the Wartburg.

I followed my companion along the brook that wound through the cleft in the mountain. As we picked our way along the slippery banks, the cliff walls rose higher and the air grew cooler. Below a jagged ribbon of sky, we were pressed into a world of running water and stark gray stone.

"Sir," I said, "do you know the stories they tell about this place?"

The knight turned to grin at me. "Are you not in the company of the dragon slayer?"

The crevice through which we threaded our way grew so narrow that the knight's shoulders brushed first one wall, then the other, as he stepped over the little torrent of the brook. A sharp turn of the path revealed a silver stream pouring down a steep cliff. We stood heedless of the mist that dampened our faces and hair. Beyond the waterfall the ravine widened slightly, and we came upon a tiny pool shimmering alongside the brook. The pool was so still that we could see the full circle of the sun undulating slowly on its surface.

Sir Georg crouched at the edge of the pool, elbows on his knees, eyes fixed on the bright reflection. I crouched beside him, and when I turned my gaze toward my companion, his head was bowed and his eyes were closed. I do not know how long he remained in silent thought or prayer, but when at last he stirred, my knees creaked stiffly as I rose.

"Ah, Seppel," the knight said dreamily, "for years I filled my days and nights with activity in my zeal to do God's will. I worked long and slept little. I ended every letter with 'yours in haste,' for even as I wrote my signature on one page I was turning my mind to the next."

He ran a hand through his cropped hair. "When I first came to the Wartburg, I felt only the absence of friends and colleagues, the loss of the accustomed rhythms of my life. Now I understand that this is all part of a greater plan. I have been brought into the wilderness to learn God's will."

Sir Georg nodded toward the pool. "Can you understand, Seppel, that God's Word is like the sun? In a still pond we see it clearly, and its light warms the water. But in the rushing current we cannot see it as well, nor can it warm that water."

The knight's eyes glistened. "When we wish to be illumined and warmed, we must go to where we may be still. There we can see clearly. Surely then our hearts will be filled with fire and light."

"Amen," said a voice from the other side of the pool.

Sir Georg and I looked up to see a monk in a coarse brown cowl, his cheekbones as sharp as the cliff behind him.

Sir Georg rose to his feet. "The Lord be with you."

"And also with you," said the monk. "Noble sir, you are very well-spoken."

Sir Georg smiled. "If I am, it is with the help of God."

"If only those within the church could make the Word so plainly understood."

The knight nodded. "Too often the message of the Gospel is perverted. Listeners are led to believe that salvation lies in their own works."

I was quite certain that Captain von Berlepsch would end such a conversation quickly. "Sir Georg, the captain is expecting us at the castle."

But the monk asked a question, and the knight responded eagerly. Soon I was listening to a passionate discussion of salvation by grace alone. The two men's voices echoed from the cliff walls as we retraced our steps to where the horses were tied.

I led the chestnut over to Sir Georg, who was saying earnestly, "The simple and nourishing message of the Gospel—this is what the people must hear. That is what our Lord meant when he said three times to Peter, 'Feed my sheep.'"

The monk nodded. "That's precisely what Doctor Luther said when he preached at Erfurt just before he disappeared."

I stood beside the knight and held the stirrup for him. "Sir, the hour grows late."

Sir Georg swung clumsily into the saddle. "And did not Luther also speak of the wicked teachers who feed the sheep as the butchers do on Easter eve?"

The monk's jaw slackened in the gaunt face. When he spoke, his voice was little more than a whisper. "*Herr Doktor* Luther, can it be—"

Instantly my sword was out, the blade aimed at the monk's throat. "How dare you call my master by the name of an outlaw—and a commoner?"

The monk stammered, "I meant no offense, young sir."

I made my voice as steely as the captain's. "You are to beg his pardon at once."

"Forgive me, sir." The monk spoke to the knight, but he kept his eyes on me.

"Enough." Turning disdainfully from the monk, I sheathed my sword, took up the reins, and swung up onto Tintenfleck. "Truly, Sir Georg, we must take our leave."

"You are quite right, Seppel," came the meek reply.

CHAPTER 14

A Letter from Court

Sir Georg and I rode away from the Dragon's Gorge in a silence that soon grew unbearable. I waited for the knight to give some hint as to whether he was angry or disappointed or relieved. The only sounds were the calling of birds and the thud of hooves on the forest trail. At last I cleared my throat. "Doctor Luther?"

The knight turned in the saddle and reined in his horse so that Tintenfleck pulled up alongside. "Why do you call me that?"

"I know that is your name, sir."

The dark eyes searched my face. Then the knight smiled. "You have lifted a great burden from me. Now I can put off this ridiculous attire."

"Sir, you must keep your disguise, and—and I'm afraid we must tell the captain."

Sir Georg sighed. "I feel like a truant schoolboy who has been found out."

"Then we're both truant, sir, for I failed in my duty to keep you safe."

"Failed, Seppel? On the contrary, your outraged nobility quite terrified that poor monk. He will not dare to speak of what he has seen."

I was not convinced that the captain would share Sir Georg's opinion. We traveled the rest of the way in glum silence.

After Otto let us into the castle and we stabled the horses, the knight and I climbed the stairs of the Ritterhaus to the gateroom. Master Klüglein squawked an ill-tempered greeting, but the captain was nowhere in sight.

Sir Georg beckoned me to the table. "Sit down, Seppel. You deserve to hear the whole story. Your Lord of Parrots and I first met on a dark road not far from here. Late one night he and two comrades forced me from my wagon and abducted me. They put me on horseback and escorted me to the Wartburg. The world was left to wonder what had become of the notorious Martin Luther."

He pushed aside the rolled documents. "I was kept completely hidden until I had hair and beard enough not to be recognized as a monk. The captain saw to it that I was clothed like a knight. Then he set himself the difficult task of teaching me to walk and talk and carry a sword like a nobleman instead of a miner's son."

Sir Georg held out his sturdy hands, palms up. "Unlike you, Seppel, I am a commoner. My father began as a laborer in the copper mines of Thuringia. His hard work paid for my education. Before I entered the university at Erfurt, I was a student at St. Georg's School in Eisenach."

He rose and walked to the window. "The happiest years of my life were spent within sight of the Wartburg. I was an able student, and I wanted to make my father proud. On holidays my schoolmates and I hiked in the forest or made music together. When we sang in four parts, the townsfolk gave us coins or invited us to break bread in their homes."

We heard the tread of boots on the stairs. Captain von Berlepsch entered the room and tossed his cloak onto a bench. "I trust that you enjoyed your excursion."

Sir Georg turned from the window to face him. "My dear host, I must confess that I have not been altogether discreet."

"Speak plainly."

"I was recognized in the Dragon's Gorge."

The captain glanced at me. "Who would accost a knight on horseback?"

"I was on foot, Captain, discussing some points of theology."

The captain struck the table with his fist. "*Bei allen Heiligen*!" He turned to me. "Wait outside."

Before the door closed behind me, I heard the captain say, "Tell me, *Herr Doktor*, how is it that the most brilliant thinker in Germany is also the greatest fool?"

I felt my face turn as red as if the question had been addressed to me. If the captain spoke so scathingly to a hero of the people, what bitter words would he have for me?

When I was summoned back to the gateroom, the captain said, "Sir Georg tells me that you acquitted yourself well today." Then his eyes narrowed. "He also tells me that you know him by another name."

"Yes, sir."

"There are some who would pay dearly for such knowledge. What do you intend to do with this information?"

"Do, sir?" Did the captain imagine I might report the outlaw's whereabouts to the authorities? Again I felt my face grow hot. Setting my jaw, I said, "I intend to help Sir Georg remember to act more like a knight."

Captain von Berlepsch studied my face for what seemed a very long time. "Then see that you do so, young Burkhardt. See that you do."

Over the next few days I had no lessons in the armory. Once the captain left the castle with an armed band of horsemen. Twice I watched as liveried messengers were escorted into the courtyard and sent directly up to the gateroom. One day a traveling minstrel, an enormously tall man with a shock of wild hair and a harp slung over his back, entered the Wartburg on foot. The goose girl and the stableboy and even the old gardener left their tasks to cluster about him. The musician unslung his harp and sang a lively song that set the goose girl to dancing, her bare feet kicking up little swirls of dust.

When a soldier called from the door of the Ritterhaus, the harper finished his song with a flourish. Bowing to the goose girl, he said with a grin, "Your master calls a different tune." He sauntered across the courtyard and followed the soldier up the stairs.

Later that day the captain ordered me to carry a thick oilskin-wrapped bundle to Sir Georg's room. The knight set down his quill and reached eagerly for the package. I watched him unfold the oilskin to reveal two sealed letters, a rolled sheaf of pages, and several bound volumes. Sir Georg hummed cheerfully as he looked at the books. Then he unrolled the sheaf to reveal an elaborate title above printed columns of text.

"You see, Seppel," he said, peering closely at the page, "we cannot allow the message of the Gospel to be obscured by poor preaching—or by poor scholarship. Here is the printed edition of my explanations of the Scriptures. These pages will prove great help for those who prepare sermons."

I leaned in to examine the document. How amazing to think that the words written by a man hidden away in a mountaintop castle could be shared with readers in Germany and the lands beyond. Even more amazing was the transformation of ink scratched by a quill pen into these perfect blocks of type on the page. What a privilege to have a part in the making of things of such beauty and power.

Sir Georg picked up one of the letters. He was about to break the seal when he suddenly turned over the letter and looked curiously at the inscription. "Josef Burkhardt?"

I saw my own name on the letter.

The knight looked at me with wonder in his eyes. "Why does my Spalatin write to you?"

I broke the seal and unfolded the letter. Some instinct prompted me to read the words aloud.

> My dear nephew,
>
> Captain von Berlepsch informs me that you are well and prospering. He is pleased with your careful attention to his teaching and your courteous service to Sir Georg. Perhaps you are disappointed that your work consists of simple tasks instead of glorious deeds. Perhaps you are distressed that you are required to <u>keep silence</u> when you are eager to speak. Good Sir Georg often reminds me that not only priests, but all believers are called to serve God. We are called to perform our duties willingly and well, <u>for in serving others we serve our Lord.</u>

The knight stared at me. "You? You are a Burkhardt of Spalt?" Shaking his head, he said, "So the nephew of Spalatin is a fellow exile in the Kingdom of the Birds."

He looked down at his knightly garb, then at my own fine attire. "As I recall, the Burkhardts were a family of tanners." Sir Georg grinned. "My dear Seppel, you are as great a pretender as I!"

At the evening meal in the gateroom Sir Georg said indignantly, "Captain, why did you not tell me that Seppel was the nephew of Spalatin?"

The captain grimaced. "When you were not aware of the boy's parentage, you were not tempted to reveal your own. Spalatin and I agreed that a commoner pretending to be a knight would best be served by a commoner pretending to be a page. Any son of rank would have pierced your thin disguise long ago."

He turned to me. "You may recall that loyal subjects of the emperor are commanded not to lodge or shelter this outlaw. Neither by words nor deeds are they to offer this man any form of assistance." With a glance at the knight, the captain added, "When the boy was ignorant of the truth, he could not be accused of conspiring against the emperor. "

Sir Georg looked troubled. "I do not wish to bring harm upon him—or you, Captain, or any of those who have been kind to me."

A long silence followed. At last I understood that the two men were waiting for me to speak.

"I am called to serve you both," I said. "I will continue to do so, whatever the risk."

The captain exhaled in a snort of exasperation or contempt. "Those are brave words, young Burkhardt, but none of us knows how this game will play out. Even Duke Frederick himself, who made the decision to provide refuge, does not know where this man is hidden. He left the matter completely in your uncle's hands."

"Spalatin spoke to me in Worms," said Sir Georg. "He told me only that I would be taken prisoner before I could return to Wittenberg." The knight raised his tankard. "The Burkhardts are my guardian angels."

"If only you had an army of angels," said the captain, "and a sense of self-preservation."

Sir Georg smiled. "The Lord will preserve me until such time as he chooses to call me home."

The captain sighed. "Yes, but if you are called home on my watch, my position will be considerably less than comfortable."

The next morning in his chamber Sir Georg said, "Now, Seppel, what reply will you make to your uncle?"

"Reply, sir?"

"He has written you, has he not? Now you must write him back. That is the meaning of correspondence."

The knight cleared away his own half-finished page and laid a new sheet of paper on the table. "I could not tolerate my exile without the pleasure of exchanging letters with friends. Sit down, Seppel."

I sat in Sir Georg's chair, and he pulled up the stool beside me. "You must write your uncle in Latin, of course. He will be pleased to note your progress."

"I—I do not know much Latin, sir."

"Then I will teach you. What a blessing that God has sent us here. We have much to do, Seppel. You must see to your correspondence. I shall ask the captain to fetch us a Latin grammar."

I picked up the quill. "But, sir, how will this letter get to my uncle?"

"The captain sends all of my correspondence to Spalatin. Whom else should you write? Have you sent any letters to your mother?"

"My mother cannot read, sir."

"That matters not," said the knight. "If she were to receive a letter from her beloved son, she would rejoice like the widow who found the lost coin. She would call in the neighbors and find one who could read. A mother would make that neighbor read the lines over and over until she had them by heart."

In my mind I saw Mother clutching a letter, her lips moving as she repeated words I had written. I imagined her fingers tracing the lines as lovingly as she might caress my face. As happened so often when I thought of home, I reached to touch the little pouch I wore under my tunic.

Then I set down the quill.

"Sir Georg, my mother asked me to find a priest to say a Mass for my father's soul. You're a priest, sir. Might you be able to do that? I have money to pay you." As soon as the words were out, I wished I could take them back. How crass to offer this great man a handful of coins.

Sir Georg did not take offense. "Your mother's faith is quite touching. However, dear Seppel, no prayers or Masses can have any effect on the souls of the dead. A private Mass is itself a subversion of our Lord's intentions. I have written at length on this matter. No priest should accept payment for such an act. For too long, the hard-earned coins of German housewives have poured into the coffers of Rome. Do you understand?"

"Yes, sir."

I was not at all sure that I did. The coins weighed heavily in the little pouch.

> Dear Mother,
>
> I hope this letter finds you well. Give my love to Renata, Ludmilla, and Annchen, and greet all our neighbors in Spalt. I have learned to ride my horse very well and to fight with a sword. The lady of the castle has taught me to play the lute. I say my prayers every night and think of you often.
>
> With great affection,
>
> Your son, Seppel

CHAPTER 15

A Hunting Party

Sir Georg wasted no time in improving my Latin. The next day I was conjugating verbs and copying translations in my neatest hand. The knight opened his big Latin Bible to a book of the New Testament. "In his letter to the Ephesians, the Apostle Paul has provided a lesson for Christian knights. Translate these lines, if you please, beginning just here."

"Therefore, put on the armor of God," I said slowly, "that you may stand in all things perfect." I looked blankly at Sir Georg. "What does it mean to 'stand perfect'?"

"In a literal translation one loses the warrior image. We Germans would say it thus: 'that you may overcome and hold the field.' Now read from here."

"And take unto you—*galeum salutis*—the helmet of salvation—*et gladium Spiritus*—and the sword of the Spirit—*quod est verbum Dei*—which is the Word of God."

"Excellent, Seppel. With such weapons the Christian is well-armed indeed."

A few days later Sir Georg and I were summoned to the gateroom. Captain von Berlepsch paced the floor while Master Klüglein rasped and clucked to himself on the perch.

"According to my sources," said the captain, "it is rumored that Luther is holed up in Thuringia. Sir Georg, we must hide you in plain sight." He rubbed his hands together briskly. "I have arranged to join a hunting party near the Castle Altenstein. I want our neighbors to see you engaged in knightly pursuits."

Sir Georg frowned. "I do not think I would enjoy the hunt."

"You are a nobleman. Without question you will enjoy the hunt."

"Captain, I have very little in common with the local aristocracy."

"I understand that. However, a knight may neglect the chase if he is a charming companion to the ladies."

Sir Georg looked alarmed. "I have very little experience in that area."

"That matters not. I have decided that you are to become a suitor for my daughter."

The knight and I both stared at the captain in horror.

He frowned. "Your interest in my daughter will explain your extended stay at the Wartburg."

"I beg your pardon, Captain," said the knight, "but I have no interest—I mean of that kind—in your daughter."

"Do you imagine I want an outlawed priest for a son-in-law? This is merely a stratagem. Your desire to remain near Ilse will explain your forgoing the company of the men. The plan is brilliant in its simplicity."

That evening Hermina was eager to share what she had overheard. "What a frightful scene there was," she told Otto and me. "First the captain said that Ilse was to welcome the attentions of Sir Georg. Then Ilse said she could never welcome his attentions, and then the captain said she was to obey orders, and then she said she was neither a soldier nor a servant, and then he said—"

When Hermina paused for breath, Otto glanced at me. "What do you think of Sir Georg as a husband for *Fräulein* Ilse?"

I could not tell whether Otto knew the knight's true identity. Never by word or deed had he ever indicated that Sir Georg was anything other than a nobleman.

I said, "It's difficult to think of any man as a husband for *Fräulein* Ilse."

Hermina laughed and ruffled my hair. "I must go back upstairs. Who knows what might happen next!"

On the morning of the hunt Captain von Berlepsch, Sir Georg, Ilse, and I rode out of the Wartburg at dawn. Ilse was surprisingly cheerful, and she conversed easily with her father and the knight. As usual, she ignored me, but I was content to ride a little distance behind my companions with the pack horse trailing behind me.

I amused myself by practicing my Latin as we rode along: "*Cum puella beata est, bella est.* When the girl is happy, she is pretty."

We had traveled nearly an hour through the green depths of the forest when I smelled wood smoke and burning grease and heard the clanking of metal and the yelp of dogs. Shafts of light pierced the canopy of leaves, and through the branches I could glimpse blue sky. The path widened, and we rode out into a wide clearing at the foot of a hill.

I blinked in the bright sunshine and saw a world teeming with colors and movement and noise. An enormous pavilion stood in the middle of the clearing, the blue and white striped walls of the tent billowing gently. I saw clusters of noblemen in hunting attire of russet and scarlet and green. Several cooking fires were burning, each tended by a servant to stir the pot. A row of horses was tethered along the edge of the clearing, black and brown and white tails all switching at flies.

A pack of hounds rose up to greet our approach. Barking hoarsely, they bounded up to us, circling our horses and panting, tongues lolling between their yellow teeth. A blast from a horn summoned them, and the dogs turned, tumbling over one another in their eagerness to return to the man with the horn. The hounds crouched at his feet, nervous and alert.

Beside the master of the hounds stood the big-bellied nobleman we had once met in the forest. Lord Hund von Wenkheim approached us, took off his feathered cap, and smiled at Ilse. "Could this fine lady be the red-headed wildcat my son remembers from two summers ago?"

Demurely Ilse allowed him to help her down from her horse. "How is Peter? Is he still enrolled at Erfurt?"

Lord Hund von Wenkheim sighed, "As far as I know." He turned to Sir Georg. "My son thinks that the nobility ought to be well-educated. I fear he neglects the hunt and other more lordly pursuits."

"Your son is at university?" said the knight with interest. "What does he study?"

"Drinking songs, I suspect. He fancies himself a scholar and has been rechristened with a ridiculous Latin name."

Sir Georg turned to me. "How do you suppose one would translate 'Hund von Wenkheim' into Latin?"

A serving-woman curtseyed before Ilse and escorted her to the pavilion. When the flap of the doorway was pulled aside, I heard the voices of women and the ripple of a lute.

A groom helped me tether the horses. Then I found Captain von Berlepsch and Sir Georg seated with Lord Hund von Wenkheim and some other men at a rough-hewn table under a spreading oak, trenchers and tankards before them. I stood near the servants, hoping that someone would think to offer me food and drink.

Lord Hund von Wenkheim said, "Tell me, Georg, how do you find life at the Wartburg?"

"I am quite content. Hans von Berlepsch is an excellent host."

"Surely you must think the days tedious after the life to which you were accustomed."

Sir Georg smiled. "We go where God calls us. I welcome the opportunities the Wartburg has provided." He nodded toward the pavilion.

The lord chuckled. "I think I understand."

"I hope you will excuse me from the chase," said Sir Georg, "if I may be of service to those who remain in camp."

A short time later, when Lord Hund von Wenkheim signaled to the master of the hounds, a flurry of activity ran through the camp. Grooms fetched horses, a dozen commoners picked up leather drums or long pikes, and the ladies came out of the pavilion. Sir Georg strode at once to the noblewomen and bowed deeply. I saw Ilse performing introductions and watched her take the knight's arm as he conversed with the ladies. In the meantime the men mounted their horses while the dogs kept circling, whining with excitement.

Servants carried stools and tapestries to a shaded spot a little way up the hill. I followed Sir Georg and the ladies and assisted the servants in spreading the tapestries over the grass. One of the servants handed Sir Georg a lute.

From the hillside we watched a dozen men and boys fan out across the field. At a blast from the horn, these beaters strode through the long grass, pounding the drums. Flocks of birds exploded from the ground, but the master of the hounds kept the dogs in check. Something brown flashed upward—a hare. Another sprang up, and a third. The master released the dogs, first the fleet-footed sighthounds, then the thick-jawed harriers.

With a glad shout Lord Hund von Wenkheim raised his feathered cap, and a line of horsemen plunged out into the field.

Ilse sat with her hands folded in her lap, but her chin was high and her eyes were on the scene below.

Sir Georg glanced at her. "*Fräulein* Ilse, would you prefer to join the hunt?"

She did not look at him. "My father wishes me to keep you company."

Setting aside the lute, the knight said, "I have a sudden urge to get a closer view of the hunt. Would you like to ride with me?"

A smile transfigured Ilse's face. At Sir Georg's request I fetched the horses.

Soon we were riding toward the sounds of horns and shouts of men. Eisblume swept ahead, and Sir Georg and I watched the white mare growing smaller in the distance. The smooth terrain became more rugged, and, when Tintenfleck swerved to avoid saplings and briars, I leaned into the turns with exhilaration, proud of my skill. We jumped a narrow stream, and I nearly lost my cap.

A hare sprang almost directly beneath us. Tintenfleck sidestepped, and abruptly I was half out of the saddle, clutching at horsehair and leather. Away bounded the hare, appearing and disappearing and appearing again in magnificent leaps over the grass.

Further on, we thundered past three huntsmen on foot, who carried long pikes from which several dead hares swung. Sir Georg slowed the chestnut to a trot, and I reined in Tintenfleck.

"I have little desire to be in on the kill," said the knight. "Ride on, Seppel." He gestured toward some nearby trees. "I will wait here for your return."

I let my horse have his head, and we charged toward the sound of men and dogs. Tintenfleck was lathered with sweat when we reached the main body of the hunting party. Netting had been strung over the briars at the edge of the forest. A score of unfortunate hares was thrashing wildly in the snare, dangling in a grotesque dance. The master of the hounds kept the dogs in check while the huntsmen moved in with their sharp pikes. Listening to the shrieks of the dying, I wished I had remained in camp.

When I returned to the trees where I had left Sir Georg, I found him sitting on the grass reading a book. The chestnut was grazing nearby. Looking around to be sure that no one else could see my lord in such an unknightly position, I led Tintenfleck over to the tree and looped the reins around a branch.

Sir Georg set his book on the cloak that lay beside him. The folds of scarlet shifted under his hand.

"Look out, sir! Something is under your cloak."

"*Ach*, Seppel, I have rescued one of the victims of this so-called pleasure of heroes. Look here."

Gently he pulled back the edge of the cloak to reveal a patch of brown fur. A half-grown rabbit lay sprawled on the lining, sides heaving, eyes glazed with pain or fear. Sir Georg sighed and covered the creature again.

"Is this not the way that our Savior rescues us from the traps and snares of false teachers and evil counselors? How helpless we are to escape a cruel fate without his powerful, loving hand."

I heard the faint notes of a horn. Crouching next to the knight, I spoke slowly and carefully. "Sir Georg, what do you intend to do with this rabbit?"

"I had not thought that far ahead."

The brush rustled and three hounds trotted out from the trees, tongues lolling, tails wagging lazily. Abruptly Sir Georg thrust the book inside his doublet and reached for the folded cloak. He rose to his feet, staggering a little, clutching the bundle as if it were an infant.

The dogs smelled the rabbit—instantly their ears pricked and the trot turned into a purposeful lope straight toward the knight. Sir Georg drew his sword and brandished it against the dogs who began to circle, growling and snapping at him. In turns the animals made little rushes at the knight, stopping just short of the length of the blade.

"Get back, whelp of Satan!" Sir Georg shifted the bundle, and the hare's head popped out from the scarlet folds. The dogs barked savagely, the terrified hare wriggled free, hit the ground, and made one desperate leap before the dogs were upon it. Ferociously the knight struck at the dogs with the flat of his blade, but they were too quick for him. One vicious shake broke the rabbit's neck, and then the hounds fought over their quarry, tugging and tearing at their prize.

At the call of the horn the hounds abandoned their game and loped away into the woods. Sir Georg knelt in the grass and stared at the bloodied corpse with tears in his eyes. "Is it not ever thus? How easily even souls that have been saved can be snatched by the powers of darkness."

In the camp that evening Sir Georg had little appetite for the hunters' feast. He sat at the far end of the table and smiled ruefully when other men made jokes at his expense.

"*Fräulein* von Berlepsch," said one of the noblemen, "what do you think of a man who has no stomach for hunting?"

Ilse lifted her chin. "Perhaps he concerns himself with higher matters."

Lord Hund von Wenkheim guffawed. "Well said, well said indeed! Sir Georg has the heart of a poet, does he not? Let us drink to the poets, my friends, for this world needs poets as well as hunters."

As I refilled Sir Georg's tankard, the knight murmured, "He too was one of my abductors. Am I not indeed protected by a powerful and loving hand?"

"Yes, sir," I said. "*Ergo, cogita ante salis.* Therefore, think before you leap."

Sir Georg chuckled. "*Bene dixit*, Seppel. Well said."

CHAPTER 16

The Royal Visit

One evening in early September, Hermina hurried to find Otto and me downstairs in the palace. "We're to have a royal visitor! Duke Johann is coming! The elector himself is coming to the Wartburg!"

Picturing the nearly empty rooms of the palace, I said, "Why would he want to come here?"

Hermina was shocked. "The Duke of Saxony is also the Landgrave of Thuringia. Of course he must visit the ancient Thuringian high court." She turned to Otto. "You've seen his Grace, haven't you? Is he grand? What does he look like?"

Otto shrugged. "He looks like a man who enjoys a good dinner."

"Why I put up with you I don't know." Hermina flounced away, and Otto winked at me. In such moments the residents of the castle were little different from the villagers of Spalt.

The following day Captain von Berlepsch summoned Sir Georg and me to the gateroom. "No doubt you have heard that Duke Johann of Saxony is to visit the Wartburg. We will have much traffic in and out of the castle." He eyed Sir Georg sternly. "It is imperative that you do not call undue attention to yourself. Have you ever spoken to his Grace?"

"I have never been introduced to him, Captain, but he has heard me preach."

"As neither he nor his brother, Duke Frederick, is to know your whereabouts, I cannot have you recognized by a tradesman or a courtier." The captain looked thoughtful. "However, you must attend the royal feast. The visiting nobility and the townspeople of Eisenach must see Sir Georg as an ordinary knight."

"Did you wish me to escort *Fräulein* Ilse?"

"I hardly think so. I remember the hunting party all too well." More gently the captain added, "How goes the writing?"

Sir Georg smiled. "Very well, Captain. I have recently been able to—"

"Good, good." The captain waved a hand in dismissal. "You may return to your scribbling."

As I followed the knight out of the room, the captain said, "Young Burkhardt!"

"Yes, sir?"

"Sir Georg is not to be seen carrying a book. He is not to converse with anyone except the members of my household. Do I make myself clear?"

"Yes, sir."

The next morning I waited outside the kitchen until Gunda glanced up from the chopping block and growled, "What do you want?"

"The captain orders you come to the gateroom."

"I have work to do. Tell him to come to me."

I stood there in confusion, reluctant to repeat the captain's order to the cook or to report the cook's answer to the captain.

When Gunda glared at me again, I retreated to the courtyard. Slowly I climbed the stairs to the gateroom.

The captain cursed. "Who is the master here? Tell her—no, wait. I will tell her myself." He stomped down the stairs and out into the yard.

This was an encounter I did not want to miss. Following at a safe distance, I stood under the pear tree's drooping branches, which were heavy with ripening fruit.

"Gunda!" shouted the captain. "Gunda, come here at once!"

The figure of the cook filled the doorway, her face glowering above the bloodstained apron.

Captain von Berlepsch said icily, "The lord of the Castle Altenstein has agreed to send his kitchen staff to prepare a feast in honor of Duke Johann's visit. You will assist them as needed."

Gunda folded her arms across her chest. "At the Wartburg I am the cook."

"This is no simple task," said the captain. "Such an occasion requires expertise beyond the ordinary meals of the household."

"I was born at the Wartburg," said Gunda. She stared at the captain as if those words should end the discussion.

The captain frowned. "Neither you nor I can afford to displease the Elector of Saxony."

Gunda's stony expression did not change. "I was born at the Wartburg. I will die at the Wartburg."

The captain's face turned red, and his jaw was tight. "Gunda," he said, speaking very distinctly, "At the Wartburg I am the master."

"And I am the cook."

"*Bei allen Heiligen!*" The words echoed against the kitchen wall. "Listen to me, you stubborn woman. Even if I were to permit you to serve as head cook, how could you possibly prepare such a feast on your own?"

Gunda stared him down. "A good master can always find good help."

Abruptly the captain turned his head and stared out across the courtyard. Instinctively I shrank back against the trunk of the tree.

Then Captain von Berlepsch faced the cook once more. "Return to your work at once. When I send the requirements for the feast, you will follow my orders exactly."

Gunda unfolded her arms. "Very good, sir."

Later that day I was summoned to the chamber where Lady von Berlepsch was reclining with her eyes closed. Ilse sat gazing out of the window, toying with her lute. Without any form of greeting, Dame Adela said, "We are in need of a scribe. Captain von Berlepsch tells me that you have a neat hand."

At her direction I removed the chessboard from the little table and took a quill pen, inkwell, and paper from a side drawer.

Without looking toward the window, Dame Adela said, "Ilse, if you are ever to learn how to manage a household, you ought to put aside that lute and come over here."

Ilse sighed heavily as she took a seat beside me.

I dipped the quill into the inkwell and wrote according to Dame Adela's dictation:

A roast of venison
Pies of fine mutton
Geese in a dish with a sorrel sauce
A roast pig with an apple sauce
A double rib of beef roasted with a sauce of vinegar
A loin of veal with a mustard sauce
A rack of lamb
Capons roasted with a sauce of wine and salt

Dame Adela turned to Ilse. "What seems to be missing?"

I turned the paper slightly to offer her a better angle for reading.

Ilse shrugged. "I have no idea."

"Roasted hare," said Lady von Berlepsch without opening her eyes. "Also pigeons and quail and a dish of songbirds."

Obediently I added those items to the list.

"Ilse, what shall we have for sweets?" prompted Dame Adela.

Ilse said with what I suspected was false cheer, "Why, tarts, gingerbread, and honeycakes, of course."

I looked at Dame Adela, who nodded. I could feel Ilse's baleful eyes on me as I wrote the last line.

Dame Adela looked over the menu. "I told Hans we should bring in the head cook and the staff from the Castle Altenstein, but he insists we use Gunda with hired help from Eisenach." She sniffed. "His loyalty to her is ridiculous."

I ducked my head so that neither she nor Ilse could see me smile.

In the Ritterhaus the following morning, Sir Georg and I stood at a window overlooking the courtyard. A donkey train was lined up head to tail along the castle wall. The sturdy little animals were barely visible under bulging sacks and kegs and baskets and bundles. Ewes and lambs were milling around a young shepherd, and an ox was tied near the kitchen door. Geese wandered in the courtyard, hissing when a larger animal stretched out an inquisitive muzzle. A hog had been penned in a makeshift corral near the pear tree. A pair of hunters bore a fresh-killed deer slung on a pole, and another huntsman stood with his pike loaded with hares.

One of the strangest sights was a donkey whose burden, a netted flock of songbirds, lifted and slid and rose and fell.

"Poor little singers," said Sir Georg. "Trapped like unwary souls in the snares of the evil one." Abruptly he left the window and returned to his room, closing the door so as to shut out the clamor.

On the feast day, the aroma of roasting meat and baking bread wafted through the courtyard, which was filled with townsfolk hired to assist as grooms and scullions, housemaids and lackeys. The castle grounds were as noisy and crowded as they might have been in ancient days when the Landgrave of Thuringia held court.

When the Saxon herald arrived with a pair of soldiers as an advance guard, men brushed dirt off their tunics and women adjusted their headpieces. The visiting commoners clustered in noisy little groups, often glancing toward the underpass that led to the gate. At last the cry went up: "He is coming!"

As the duke's party rode into the courtyard, the assembled men and women bowed their heads respectfully, though many of them peeked sideways so as not to miss the scene. Duke Johann was a burly rider with a thick dark beard and small eyes. His royal mount was clearly fatigued from the steep climb up the mountain. The dust of travel could not conceal the splendor of the jewel that adorned the nodding plumes of the elector's cap or the chased-silver scabbard that lay across his horse's sweaty flanks.

The captain himself held the duke's horse while his Grace dismounted with a grunt. Grooms hurried to take the horses of the courtiers and Saxon soldiers. Duke Johann raised his arm and turned slightly right, then left, to acknowledge his loyal subjects. Then the captain escorted the royal presence through the arch to the inner courtyard. The courtiers and officers followed their lord toward the palace. The Saxon soldiers established their authority by ordering the townspeople to remain in the outer courtyard.

All afternoon other guests entered the castle gate, and by dusk the stable was full of horses. Hermina found me in the front hall of the Ritterhaus. "Have you heard, Seppel? Lord Hund von Wenkheim's son Peter has not yet arrived. As the heir of the Castle Altenstein, he was to sit at the high table. His father is in a towering rage!"

Hermina was never prettier than when she was telling other people's business. "And Lady von Berlepsch is too unwell to attend, so Dame Adela is to take her place at the high table."

Hermina's face clouded. "I must attend the lady, so I can only peep in at the feast." She put her hand on my arm. "You must tell me all about it. Remember, Seppel, I want to know everything!"

That evening in the Singers' Hall, torchlight danced over the elaborate patterns on the walls. A band of hired musicians played harps and lutes and pipes and drums. I recognized the tall harper from his visits to the Wartburg. With delight I saw that the little piper was Dolf.

In the seat of honor at the high table sat his Grace, Johann, Duke of Saxony and Landgrave of Thuringia. On the duke's right sat Lord Hund von Wenkheim with his wife and a lady-in-waiting. I reminded myself to inform Hermina that no chair had been left for the absent Peter.

On the duke's left sat Dame Adela, looking very pleased with herself. The captain sat next to her with Ilse beside him. Ilse's hair was braided into a firelit crown, and jewels sparkled at her throat. I would have to tell Hermina that Ilse von Berlepsch was easily the most beautiful woman in the room.

The other tables in the hall were positioned so that all the guests had a view of the high table. At one table, the visiting courtiers leaned toward one another, speaking freely and laughing loudly. At another, the officials of Eisenach and their wives sat stiffly, conversing in subdued voices. At a third table, Sir Georg sat with the noblemen who had been among the hunting party. One of them called, "How's your appetite, Georg?" and another recommended the roasted hare. Sir Georg took their jibes with good humor and dined quite well. I myself ate so much rich food that my senses were dulled and I could hardly tell whether a sauce was mustard or sorrel or vinegar.

After the last crumbs of tarts and gingerbread and honeycakes had been cleared away, Duke Johann rose a bit unsteadily to his feet. With a great scraping of chairs and benches against the slate floor, the entire company stood as well.

"Friends and loyal subjects," said the duke, "we thank you for your generous hospitality. The Wartburg has long stood as a symbol of Thuringia's love of the arts, strength in adversity, and endeavors to reach great heights. As the Thuringians say, 'Through vigilance we climb higher.' *Vigilando ascendimus!*"

"*Vigilando ascendimus!*" The walls echoed the chorus of voices.

The duke cleared his throat and spoke less formally. "I cannot remember when I last dined so well. Where is your head cook, Captain? Bring forth the cook!"

The servants nearest the door scuttled away to do his Grace's bidding. Duke Johann sat down and signaled his guests to be seated. I wondered whether Gunda would be too busy to obey the duke's summons. Judging from the expression on the captain's face, I was not alone in entertaining that thought.

The duke's servants returned and took their places on either side of the arch. Between them stood Gunda, her face as grim as ever as she looked suspiciously around the torchlit hall. The murmur of voices died. The assembled company looked expectantly at the high table.

When Duke Johann beckoned her, Gunda crossed the silent room with a calm majesty. The firelight flickered over a spotless white apron as she stood before the high table.

The duke inclined his head. "We thank you, good *Frau*, for this fine repast. On our behalf you are to commend all those who have assisted in providing the feast."

Gunda did not move or speak. The silence stretched for so long that I wondered whether she had even heard the duke. The guests at the long tables stirred, and there were whispers among the courtiers.

Duke Johann squinted at the cook. "You have served at the Wartburg for some time, is that not so?" He glanced at the captain. "Good *Frau*, would you consider a position at the Saxon court?"

Gunda crossed her massive arms. "I was born at the Wartburg," she said. "I will die at the Wartburg. Let no fool dare to keep me from my calling."

There was a stunned silence in the Singers' Hall.

The nobleman and the cook stared at one another across the high table. Then Duke Johann chuckled. "Spoken like a true Thuringian." He raised his tankard. "Let no fools dare to keep us from our calling."

CHAPTER 17

The Tale of the Singers

Hardly had Gunda left the banqueting hall when I saw Dolf walk to Sir Georg's table. Still holding his pipe, the kitchen boy leaned to whisper to the knight, who glanced toward the high table. Then Sir Georg excused himself from his companions and followed Dolf out of the hall. I rose from my seat immediately. With so many strangers in the castle, it seemed wise to keep an eye on my lord.

I found Sir Georg standing among the musicians in the passageway.

The tall harper bowed to the knight. "Good sir, I beg pardon for disturbing you, but we are in dire need of your musical gifts. One of our number has feasted too well." He lifted an invisible cup to his lips.

"We are to enact the great Tournament of Song, and we must have one more singer for the contest. Dolf tells us that you have a fine voice and know the work of Walther von der Vogelweide. I beseech you, sir, will you play that part this night to honor his Grace in song?"

I said, "Sir, you should not—" but when the players turned to look at me, I closed my mouth.

Sir Georg smiled. "If someone would trade me a lute for this sword, I will be well pleased to join your number."

Helplessly I watched him unbuckle his sword belt and set the weapon aside. The harper gave the knight an old-fashioned tunic like the ones that he and the other players were wearing. Without hesitation the knight donned the tunic. One of the other musicians handed him a lute.

Sir Georg ran his fingers over the strings. "What would you have me play?"

"Something befitting royalty," said the harper. "Address the duke as if he is indeed the Landgrave Hermann of the old tale. We must all praise things pleasing to his Grace. The last singer will lose the contest by failing to do so."

The harper nodded toward a fair-haired young man, then said, "After I begin the telling, I will sing the role of Wolfram von Eschenbach. Sir Georg, you will be the third to sing."

The harper stepped out to the center of the hall. He swept a low bow to the high table and announced, "I am Jacoby of Austria." His deep voice carried to the farthest corners of the room. "My companions and I have come to offer the delights of music to this fair assembly."

Acknowledging the other tables, he said, "Good people, we players can give all that we have and yet be none the poorer." The harper flashed a grin. "May you be as generous when our work is done." He turned smartly, his long cloak swirling about him, and crossed the floor to stand beside the stage.

Then Jacoby of Austria began his tale: "Once in the days when the world was young, the Wartburg gleamed with new-cut stone. The castle shone like a beacon over the great forest. Wandering minstrels visited often and stayed long, for the Landgrave Hermann and his lady Sophie were warm to welcome and quick to praise."

"More than three hundred years ago, on a night such as this one, the greatest singers of the land gathered in this very hall. After a feast such as this one, when the torches were flickering and the candles were burning low, it happened that someone proposed a contest of song."

The harper's tone became musing. "Yes, a contest of song. Where better to celebrate the glory of music than here on the heights of the Wartburg?"

Jacoby strode to the table where the officials of Eisenach sat. "But a contest must have a prize. In the light of day the choice might have been clear. A heavy purse of the coin of the realm? A favor from a fair lady?"

He looked keenly up and down the table, and there was a stirring among the stout dames of Eisenach.

"But the night had been long and the cellars well-stocked, and a darker murmur began in the hall. Who can say who first began it, the notion that not the winner but the loser should be singled out?"

Jacoby shrugged. "Yes, a dark whisper went around the hall, and someone made bold to say that the loser of the contest of song would pay with his life."

The harper's face became grave. "Dear ladies, though it wrenches your gentle hearts to hear it, I must tell you that the hangman himself was summoned to this very hall." He pointed toward one of the arches.

The ladies gasped. A noose was hanging there, the thick rope coiled like an ugly snake.

"One by one, the singers took the stage to praise the Landgrave in song. The first was Wolfram von Eschenbach."

Doffing his cloak and taking up his harp, Jacoby of Austria was instantly transformed into a Minnesinger of ancient days. The strings of the harp rippled, and he began to sing of the virtues of those who live within sight of the Wartburg. All who see that mountaintop castle are inspired to live as godly a life as those who dwell at the high court of Thuringia.

Behind me, the fair-haired player murmured to Sir Georg, "Did you have good hunting the other day?"

I tried to indicate to the knight that he should put an end to the conversation.

Sir Georg shook his head. "I confess I am a better musician than I am a hunter. I did enjoy the company of those who excel in the sport."

"And was Ilse von Berlepsch one of those whose company you enjoyed?"

Eyeing the young man sharply, I said, "I believe your business here is to play music, not to question your betters."

The fair-haired player bowed deeply. "Young sir, I beg your pardon." He seemed amused rather than contrite.

Jacoby ended the song and donned his cloak again to resume his role as narrator. When the next player began a song about the joys of wandering the Thuringian Forest, I studied the young man who had spoken so boldly. He seemed more comfortable in the royal presence than did the other players.

After the second song ended, I watched the high table as Sir Georg stepped into the light. Captain von Berlepsch paused with a tankard raised to his lips. Very slowly he set down the tankard. I saw him place his hands upon the table, the familiar shift toward balance. His face strained and alert, the captain caught the eye of Otto, who stood near the royal guards. Otto's hand moved to the hilt of his sword.

Sir Georg bowed to the high table. "Most illustrious Landgrave, honored guests, I offer a song about a king's folly. Naturally, the rulers of Thuringia are too wise to repeat such a mistake."

At the sound of that voice, Ilse turned to look at her father, who steadfastly ignored her.

I watched Duke Johann as Sir Georg began to sing. Would the duke recognize the voice of the Wittenberg preacher?

> King Constantine in folly gave
> The cross, the crown, the sacred stave
> That pierced our Lord, all to the holy see.
> The angel mourned his folly so:
> "Ah woe, ah woe, ah threefold woe!
> For Christendom is now in jeopardy.
> I see a subtle poison fall
> And turn their honey into gall;
> On man a heavy burden will be laid."

Puzzling over the lines, I realized that the angel in the song was unhappy because the church had become more powerful than the state.

> The princes stripped of proper awe,
> The highest prince of power deprived
> By this election which the priests contrived.
> Let accusation before God be made:
> The clerics are perverting civil law.
> It was no falsehood that the angel said!

When the last notes died away, there was a silence in the hall. Every eye was fixed on Duke Johann. Sir Georg stood facing the duke, his hands resting upon the lute.

Duke Johann leaned back in his chair. His words were addressed to Lord Hund von Wenkheim, but he spoke for all to hear: "The singer is right, you know. Even today we are fighting the same battle." He clapped his hand sharply together.

The sound echoed against the walls. Immediately the other guests began to applaud. Sir Georg bowed to acknowledge the applause and stepped back to join the other players.

The fair-haired player whispered to the knight, "That was a strange choice. I'm the one who is to lose the contest."

The fourth player's song about the virtues of the women of Thuringia was well received.

Then Jacoby of Austria told the assembly, "Last to sing on that fateful night was Heinrich von Oftendingen."

The fair-haired singer took his place under the arch. His playing was simple, but his voice was clear and strong. As he sang of the surpassing beauty of the women of the neighboring land of Hesse, there was a flurry of movement at the high table. Lord Hund von Wenkheim's face was so red he looked as if he might explode. Ilse seemed to be seized by secret laughter.

Jacoby signaled to the other players, who moved forward into the light and began to pantomime their displeasure. As the song continued, they murmured louder and louder.

When at last the singer bowed to the high table, the voice of the harper rang out through the room, "Shame! Shame!"

Another player called out, "How dare he offer praises of a land other than Thuringia?"

"The song is a scandal!"

"He has lost the contest. He must pay the price!"

Flanked by Sir Georg and the others, the tall harper seized the young man. Together they dragged the unfortunate musician toward the noose.

"No, wait! I implore you!" cried the young man. Wrenching free from his captors, he staggered across the floor and flung himself upon his knees before Ilse, who rose from her seat in surprise. "Gracious lady," the singer gasped, "have mercy upon a desperate man. Say but a word, and you spare my life!"

As the young man gazed up at the beautiful young woman, I forgot I was watching a performance. The kneeling man bowed his head as Ilse raised her arm and draped her mantle over his fair hair.

Jacoby's voice came as if from far away: "And thus it was that the Landgravine Sophie offered her protection to Heinrich. He was granted a year and a day to bring the great sage Klingsor to the Wartburg. The musicians agreed that wise Klingsor would determine the outcome of the contest."

The harper bowed to Ilse, who lifted the mantle.

The fair-haired player looked up again before he retreated to the shadows, but Ilse kept her gaze upon Jacoby.

The harper continued: "A year and a day passed, and the great Klingsor arrived at the Wartburg. He spoke prophetic words to the guests in the Singers' Hall."

Jacoby pulled up the hood of his cloak, stretched out one hand before him, and spoke in the rasping voice of an old man:

"This night a star has risen in Hungary whose brightness shall light the world. A daughter has been born to the king. Her name shall be called Elisabeth, and she shall be given in marriage to the son of the Landgrave. She will become a saint, the wonder and consolation of Christendom."

Jacoby pushed back his hood and resumed his narrator's voice. "And here on this night there sits among us one of her lineage. Honored guests, join me now in raising a cup to Dame Adela, royal descendant of our own sainted Elisabeth of the Wartburg."

Dame Adela had never looked more smug than when all the guests, including his Electoral Grace the Duke of Saxony, stood in tribute to her. I reminded myself to be sure to share that with Hermina.

When the company was seated again, Duke Johann said, "I am told that one of the singers in the contest is more than he appears to be."

Captain von Berlepsch started suddenly in his chair.

Duke Johann waved his hand. " Let the singers come forth!"

After some whispering and rustling of garments, the five singers lined up facing the high table, standing in the order in which they had sung.

Duke Johann looked at each of them in turn. Jacoby, Sir Georg, and the fair-haired singer looked very much at ease, but the other two players shifted uncomfortably under the royal gaze.

I stole a glance at the captain. If the famous outlaw were to be found out at this gathering, what would become of the family von Berlepsch?

After an agonizingly long appraisal of the five players, Duke Johann beckoned the fair-haired singer. "You, Heinrich. Come forth."

The singer stepped forward and dropped to one knee.

Duke Johann said, "I believe that you are more than a musician."

The young man smiled. "I beg your pardon, your Grace, but you are mistaken. I am less a musician than any of the others."

"Then tell me, young player, what you are."

"Your Grace, I am a student and a son of the family Hund von Wenkheim."

Beside the duke, Lord Hund von Wenkheim wore a comical expression. He seemed unable to decide whether to be angry or pleased.

Duke Johann said, "What is your Christian name?"

"Your Grace, I was christened Peter, but at Erfurt I am known as Custodomus."

"Peter Custodomus, it was most generous of you to leave your studies to attend an old man's pleasure." Duke Johann glanced over at Ilse. "And you, *Fräulein*, in what land did a star rise on the night you were born?"

"Your Grace, I was born in Hesse."

CHAPTER 18

Tricks of the Devil

On the day after Duke Johann and his entourage departed, Ilse summoned me to the ladies' chamber and offered to teach me how to play chess. Dutifully I listened as she told me the names of the carved figures and explained how to move each one over the squares of the board. I wondered whether the doings of actual knights and bishops were as complicated as the rules of this game.

"Pawns are the weakest and least valuable pieces," said Ilse. "After all, a pawn is really nothing more than a peasant with a sword."

I glanced at her sharply, but she merely smiled and moved the white king's pawn two squares forward. "Peter Custodomus said he quite enjoyed performing with Sir Georg."

I looked over my rows of game pieces and tried to figure out how to begin. "Yes, *Fräulein*. Sir Georg also had a pleasant time at the royal feast."

I decided to copy Ilse's move by placing my king's pawn on the square adjoining hers.

Ilse pushed a bishop's pawn forward one square. "Peter said that Sir Georg has a great gift for music."

"Yes, *Fräulein*."

Again, I mirrored Ilse's move by sliding my bishop's pawn forward

Ilse's hand hovered over the board before settling again on her bishop's pawn. "Perhaps Sir Georg studied music at Erfurt." The white pawn moved up one square.

According to the little I understood about the game, I could capture that pawn by moving diagonally. I slid my first pawn over and removed the white pawn from the board.

"Well done." Ilse's voice was almost a purr.

"Thank you, *Fräulein*."

"So did he study music at Erfurt?"

"I don't know. He has never told me exactly what he studied there."

Suddenly the white queen swept across the board. "Check."

How had she done that? I stared at the carved figures in dismay. Clearly, I had a great deal to learn about the games of the nobility.

As the last days of September gave way to a mellow October, Lady von Berlepsch grew stronger. On warm days she would sit outside in the rose garden when the sun was high. The mild weather did not have such a beneficial effect on Sir Georg. He rose early and worked late, writing fretfully, then furiously, with much pacing about the room. Receiving letters, which used to delight him, now caused him to mutter and sigh.

"So much unrest," he said to me one morning. "The good folk of Wittenberg do not know whom to follow. I fear for them, Seppel. They have broken free from the snares of a devilish pope, but Satan has many faces. How can simple people know false teachers from true?"

Again he began to pace. "If only I could return, Seppel. If only I could stand alongside my friends to fight the good fight."

His steps became brisker, and the circling on the slate floor almost dizzying. At last the knight sank into his chair. "And yet, perhaps my heart's longing is but another trick of the devil. I am guilty of pride, Seppel, the sin of Satan himself. Is it not empty vanity to claim that my presence alone can win the battle? Do I not presume then to be a kind of Christ?"

He buried his head in his hands, and I could barely distinguish the words. "I am weary, so weary. In the darkest hours the devil taunts me, and I lie sleepless till dawn."

That afternoon, Otto and Hermina and I accompanied some of the servants on a nutting expedition in the forest. We were all on foot, and after the long steep descent from the mountaintop, the day felt like a return to my life as a villager, a world that seemed almost a dream. As Otto and Hermina strolled hand in hand among the trees, the castle children ran here and there, gathering as many hazelnuts as their baskets could hold. Hermina settled under a tree, skirts billowing over the leaf-strewn grass, with Otto and me on either side.

She turned to me. "Seppel, did I tell you what Duke Johann said to Ilse?"

"Hermina," said Otto, "how is it that your little nose smells out more news than anyone else's?"

She ignored him. "Duke Johann asked Ilse what she looked for in a husband, and she said, 'I do not look for a husband at all.'"

Hermina shook her head, and a few curls slipped from under her cap. "How much easier to be a village girl than a nobleman's daughter. Ilse will be married off one way or the other. I expect the captain will announce a betrothal soon."

Otto chuckled. "And will it be Sir Georg who wins her as his wife?"

"For shame, Otto, to speak so lightly of a priest." Hermina stopped abruptly and stared at me, eyes wide. Otto did not look at me, but I sensed his absolute attention.

So Otto and Hermina both knew the secret of the Wartburg. What enormous relief I felt at that moment!

I said cheerfully, "Sir Georg says that in Wittenberg, priests have begun to marry. After all, our Lord does not forbid marriage. Sir Georg says that monastic vows are works of men, and to claim that a vow of chastity or any other good work makes one worthy before God is a trick of the devil."

"You are our scholar, Seppel," Hermina said admiringly.

The words stirred a sudden longing for other voices. What was Mother doing back home in Spalt? Were Renata and Ludmilla and Annchen out in the woods today, shrieking and pelting one another with hazelnuts?

My whole world seemed bounded by the walls of the Wartburg. All my waking hours were filled with the family von Berlepsch and their servants and their secret. I felt ashamed of neglecting my own family, even if only in thought. Yet almost immediately I felt new shame for wishing to abandon the kind people here.

Hermina noticed my pensive face. "Come, Seppel, you and I can fill a basket faster than this great lout can."

Her words proved true. Later when our nutting party climbed the steep path to the Wartburg, the shadows were long and the children weary, content to allow their elders to carry the heavy baskets.

I brought a basket of hazelnuts to Sir Georg's room. The knight barely looked up from his writing. He had lit a candle to ease his eyes in the twilight. Outside, the calling of the birds had subsided. The only sound was the scratching of the quill on the paper.

"Thank you, Seppel," he said without looking up. "I must work longer hours than Satan does if I am to thwart his evil plans."

I left Sir Georg to his scribbling. Later, when I brought his evening meal, the knight turned away from the stack of pages only long enough to dip into the stew with a chunk of bread that he never did eat.

"I tell you truly, Satan is never more dangerous than when he dons the robes of a priest. The Archbishop of Mainz claims to have among his collection of relics a genuine piece of manna from the wilderness. He invites pilgrims to see for themselves—for a price—the very burning bush of Moses."

Sir Georg grimaced. "I have told Spalatin that we must protest this folly. Unfortunately, your uncle and Duke Frederick find my words too extreme for their cautious ways."

Pushing away the tray, the knight turned back to his work. "I will not let the Kingdom of the Sword corrupt the Kingdom of the Spirit. Good night, Seppel, good night."

The next morning when I carried the tray to Sir Georg's chamber, the door stood open. A chilling breeze blew through the hallway. Inside the room the window gaped wide, and the bird calls from the forest were loud and insistent.

"Sir Georg?" I stepped over the threshold. Anchored by an inkwell, a few pages fluttered on the table. Perhaps the knight had gone for an early walk, but it was unlike him to leave the window open, for the castle pigeons were apt to fly in and strut around the room.

I elbowed the papers aside and set down the tray. Peering into the dark little sleeping-chamber, I called "Sir? Sir Georg?"

The bed was empty, but as I turned away, a groan prickled the hairs on the back of my neck. The knight was crouching in a corner, clutching a burnt candle stub. His eyes were closed, and his lips were moving rapidly, but I could not distinguish the words. I hesitated to speak again.

At last Sir Georg looked up at me with bloodshot eyes. "He torments me, Seppel. All night his demons rattled those hazelnuts under my bed, and, when at last my weary body was on the verge of slumber, he sent a crashing on the stairs as if a hundred barrels were rolled from top to bottom."

The knight bared his teeth in a snarl. "I tried to laugh at him. You know that he cannot endure mirth. But last night he outwitted me by keeping me wakeful, knowing that I would brood upon my helplessness while the battle rages outside these walls."

Slowly I extended my hand, palm up. The knight let go of the candle stub, which plopped and rolled to a stop. Bowing his head, Sir Georg grasped my hand in both of his. I laid my other hand over the clenched fingers, as I might have done to comfort little Annchen. "Please, sir," I said softly. "Please come out into the light."

I remember how strangely Sir Georg walked the castle grounds that morning. His lips moved, and occasionally he uttered words in German or Latin. The knight was always cordial to the servants, but today he passed the goose girl without even a nod. Following at a little distance, I made a point of smiling at her as she stared forlornly after him.

Sir Georg's path led us under an ivy-covered arch into the garden where Lady von Berlepsch sat alone, lit by the swath of sunlight that slanted over the roof of the palace.

The knight started as if from sleep. "I beg your pardon, my lady. I do not mean to intrude."

Lady von Berlepsch smiled. "I welcome your company." She gestured toward the clusters of white blossoms along the wall. "Every year at the Wartburg I am surprised to see these late roses. They seem so frail, yet they are so strong."

"My chosen emblem is a rose," said Sir Georg.

"Then bring one to me, if you please, and tell me about your emblem."

Sir Georg took out the little knife he used for preparing quills. Neatly he cut a sprig of the pale flowers and sat down on the grass beside Lady von Berlepsch.

"The white rose signifies the joy and comfort of faith," he said. "Within the rose is a red heart, for one who believes from the heart is justified. Within the heart a black cross reminds us that our saving faith comes from the one who was crucified for us." He traced the petals with his finger. "The rose is surrounded by a field of sky-blue to remind us of the heavenly joy that awaits us."

The lady said gently, "I find great comfort in the message of this rose. Are you not also comforted by this emblem of yours?"

The knight shifted his position on the grass. "I do not sleep well. I am troubled by visions."

"Are these dreams that you speak of?"

"I wake from frightening dreams to confront evil visions."

Lady von Berlepsch sighed. "Yet white roses and blue skies are all around you. You should spend more hours in a garden and fewer at your desk. And you must certainly make more music. I was sorry to miss your performance during the royal visit."

"Thank you, my lady. It is true that both mirth and music can drive away evil."

"I know another thing which the evil one cannot endure."

"What is that, my lady?"

"*Herr Doktor*, you would do well to remember that Satan cannot endure a good marriage."

I blinked. Had I really heard Lady von Berlepsch reveal the identity of her famous guest?

Sir Georg shook his head. "Dear lady, I am outlawed by pope and emperor. I could never ask a woman to share my fate. Then, too, I am not suited for marriage. What woman would have a man like me?"

Lady von Berlepsch smiled. "You demean yourself. Many a woman would be pleased to have such a godly man as her life's companion."

"I fear you hardly know me or the temptations I suffer. "

"And I fear you are too much alone. You must dine with my family, *Herr Doktor*. We shall expect you this evening."

CHAPTER 19

The Tale of the Saint

On the evening of that first meal at the family table, I brushed
the dust from Sir Georg's boots as he picked a few pigeon feathers
from his scarlet tunic. Then we descended the turning staircase of the
Ritterhaus.

Otto opened the door to the dining hall. The long banqueting table
was pushed against the wall at the far end of the room. The family
was seated near the fireplace, the captain at the head of the table,
Lady von Berlepsch on his right, Dame Adela on his left. Beside Lady
von Berlepsch, Ilse seemed to be hiding a smile as her eyes flickered
carelessly over me.

As Otto showed the knight to the seat opposite the captain, I
remained standing, unsure of what to do. Did a page sit at the table
with his lord?

The captain said, "Young Burkhardt, you are to assist in serving."

Gratefully I escaped to the corridor where Hermina was waiting
for Dolf to bring the first course. When I carried in a covered dish, I
saw Dame Adela sitting stiffly, her lips a thin line. The captain wore a
wary expression. Ilse's brow was furrowed.

Lady von Berlepsch said, "Georg, I am so glad you will be here
with us to celebrate the feast of Saint Elisabeth."

Sir Georg looked uncomfortable. "I hope this saint's day does not
include viewing of relics or other thievish tricks of popery."

Dame Adela peered at him sharply. "Who are you to question our
traditions? The people of Eisenach are never more pious than when
they pray to Elisabeth on her holy day."

The knight sighed. "Such folly should be discouraged. This long-
dead mortal cannot intervene on anyone's behalf. Only our Lord Jesus
Christ can do that."

Captain von Berlepsch cleared his throat. "Georg, I fear you
concern yourself too much with matters unbecoming a knight."

"Captain, you know as well as I do that one might as well pray to a stick or a stone as to a saint."

Lady von Berlepsch said swiftly, "Gunda will bake hundreds of loaves for the celebration. Each year a maiden of Eisenach is chosen to play the Landgravine Elisabeth. She comes out of the castle gates to give bread to the poor. When her husband the Landgrave accuses her of stealing bread from his own stores, she opens her cloak to reveal not bread but roses." The lady smiled at Sir Georg. "White roses with hearts of red."

"The play-acting is ridiculous," said Ilse.

"How can you say so, my dear?" Lady von Berlepsch shook her head. "I remember your first *Elisabethsfest*. How you clapped your hands to see the miracle!"

"I was a child. I am no longer so easily deceived." Ilse turned to Sir Georg. "Don't you find it painful to watch commoners pretending to be nobility?"

When the knight did not answer, Ilse went on. "The entire story is absurd. If the people of Eisenach were indeed starving, why would a benevolent God waste bread by turning it into flowers?"

Dame Adela gasped and crossed herself.

The captain scowled. "It is not fitting that a young woman question such things."

Lady von Berlepsch said quickly, "Saint Martin's Day will be upon us soon. The children of Eisenach will sing in the streets, lighting their way with lanterns carved from hollowed turnips. I am told the procession is quite lovely."

Sir Georg nodded. "I know the custom. It was even so when I was—when I was a child."

Ilse leaned toward him. "I feel very little connection with my namesake Elisabeth." She smiled at the knight. "Perhaps you feel more kinship with yours."

Sir Georg chuckled. "The sainted Martin wielded a sword in an act of charity, while I wield only a pen—" He stopped.

In the silent room he took a long drink from his tankard and then stared intently into its depths.

Ilse said demurely. "I thought your name was Georg."

Another silence followed.

"Bei allen Heiligen!" said the captain. "Ilse, you are to refrain from such impertinence. How dare you question the honor of our guest?"

Ilse stared at her father, her cheeks red and her chin high. "The Lord of Parrots might deceive the world beyond the Wartburg, but within these walls must we continue this absurd pretense?"

The captain's eyes were as narrow as his daughter's. "Were you not of noble blood, I would have you whipped for your insolence."

Ilse drew herself up proudly. "Like *Herr Doktor* Luther, I submit only to the authority of my Lord Jesus Christ."

The captain's glare met the startled face of the knight.

Captain von Berlepsch placed both hands on the table as if bracing himself. "We will have no further discussion of theology at this table."

He looked at each of the women in turn. "While this man is under my protection, he is to be called Georg." To Ilse, he said very quietly, "If you are as clever as you think you are, you will obey without question. Do I make myself clear?"

Ilse avoided the piercing gaze. "Yes, Father."

Then the captain looked at me. "What is spoken at this table travels no further. Do I make myself clear?"

I looked him straight in the eye. "Yes, sir."

CHAPTER 20

Of Beggars and Bread

Every November on St. Martin's Day and six days later on the feast of St. Elisabeth, I remember my time at the Wartburg. That year *Martinstag* dawned cold and damp, and Sir Georg did not leave his room. After I had tended his fire, he wrote steadily all day, occasionally rising to pace and mutter to himself. He might have spent the entire evening alone had I not been sent with the captain's request that the knight leave off scribbling to attend the traditional soldiers' feast.

Downstairs in the Ritterhaus the aroma of roasted goose filled the air. The soldiers of the Wartburg sat at the long banqueting table. Without the civilizing presence of women or royalty, the men drank deeply, spoke crudely, and laughed loudly.

Sir Georg did not participate in the banter about women and weapons. He did appreciate the wine that Captain von Berlepsch had ordered in honor of the day. However, when the captain signaled the servants to fill the cups a third time, Sir Georg turned his down on the table.

"Come now," said one of the soldiers. "Surely you have no objection to the best wine of the season?"

"Not at all," said Sir Georg. "The Apostle Paul writes that whatever goes into a man does not defile him. It is what comes out of a man that defiles him—drunkenness, gluttony, deceit—"

The other man laughed. "Are you a priest to whom we should confess our sins?"

The knight shook his head. "I am no more a priest than you. Are we not all called to do God's will? No priest's robe or bishop's ring, no vow or discipline gives one man spiritual authority over another. All of us in this room and in all of Christendom are a priesthood."

"Enough, Georg," said Captain von Berlepsch. "We know you have a poet's tongue. If you must speak, give us a few words in keeping with the day."

"Very well, Captain." Sir Georg rose from his seat.

"My friends, on this day we mark the feast of Saint Martin, who was a soldier like ourselves. God gives us saints not as intercessors, but as examples. What do we learn from the example of the soldier Martin? All of us remember his most famous act. Upon seeing a beggar shivering in the cold, Martin drew his sword, cut his cloak in half, and shared it with the one in need."

The knight looked up and down the long table. "How many other soldiers had already ridden past that beggar without seeing him? How many of us stride along each day wrapped in our own cares? Occupied with what appears to be our duty, we look neither to the right nor to the left. How then will we ever know whether God has other plans for us?"

For a moment Sir Georg stood in silence. "It sometimes happens that a man finds himself at a loss as to what God expects him to do." The knight glanced at the captain. "After all, a sword is hardly a suitable tool for cutting fabric. Why did not God provide our sainted Martin a tailor's shears?"

He smiled. "We must use what God has given us. In every circumstance we must look around to see how we might best serve our Lord. Like Saint Martin himself, wherever God has placed us and with whatever tools we have been given, we must never tire of seeking to know his will." He closed his eyes and bowed his head. "Amen."

The captain raised his cup. "To our brother Martin!"

"To Martin!" the soldiers chorused.

Sir Georg opened his eyes. "To the glory of God!"

On St. Elisabeth's Day, frost flowers sparkled in the round window panes. A dusting of snow lay over the courtyard, crisscrossed by the looping tracks of dogs and the delicate trails of birds. The castle gate stood open wide, and a long line of townspeople gathered in the courtyard, their cheeks and noses red with cold.

Several townspeople stood warming their hands over the coals of a brazier. At a steaming kettle suspended over another brazier, an old woman with a dipper filled bowls with a hot spiced drink. Jacoby the minstrel was playing to the crowd, singing snatches of song to young women who pretended dismay. The children were awed by the row of soldiers standing at attention with their long shiny halberds.

Under the arch of the inner courtyard stood Ilse in a long blue cloak. By request of the captain, Sir Georg and I were positioned as her escorts. Alongside us were enormous baskets piled high with small round loaves of bread, each loaf adorned with a five-petaled rose of dough.

The knight murmured, "Lady von Berlepsch tells me that in the giving of the *Rosenbrot*, the nobility are reminded of their duty." He looked out over the crowd. "It is important for those in power to show their willingness to serve those whom they are called to protect."

A priest from Eisenach blessed the baskets of bread. With great ceremony he lifted a decorated loaf and handed it to Ilse. Then she held out the loaf to one of the smallest children. When the little girl did not take the bread, the child's mother pushed her forward.

Ilse knelt to bring her face closer to the child's. "Please allow me to give this to you." She spoke as gently as she did to her white mare.

Cautiously the child reached for the bread, and Ilse straightened up and began handing out loaves to children who pressed forward to receive them.

Later she gave Sir Georg and me loaves of *Rosenbrot* as solemnly as she had given bread to the villagers. When I thanked her, I was rewarded with a smile. I wished that every day could be like St. Elisabeth's Day.

The knight raised his loaf and studied it. "God provides for us without our asking, yet our Lord teaches us to pray for our daily bread. God bestows all good things, of course, but he also expects us to do the work ourselves."

I looked out over the courtyard, glad that none of the townspeople was standing close enough to hear these remarks. At the edge of the crowd I saw a woman clutching a baby, two small children clinging to her skirt.

Taking hold of the pouch around my neck, I strode toward the little family as I pulled the cord over my head. "Here," I said to the woman, "please allow me to give this to you." I pressed the pouch into her hand and returned to my place under the arch.

Ilse stared at me. "What were you doing over there?"

"God's work."

Sir Georg smiled.

CHAPTER 21

ᛁn the Hand of God

One winter evening as I sat dozing near the little stove in Sir Georg's room, I woke to the knight's voice. "Now, my dear Seppel, you must listen to what I have written the Archbishop of Mainz." Standing in front of the stove, the knight began to read:

> Your Electoral Grace has now again erected at Halle that idol which robs poor simple Christians of their money and their souls. Your Electoral Grace will please remember the beginning, and what a horrible fire was kindled by one little spark. The whole world thought that one poor monk was too unimportant to receive the pope's attention and was undertaking an impossible task, but God directed the game to the point where the pope himself will hardly be able to straighten out this affair. One may clearly see the hand of God in this.

Sir Georg paced the room, his voice charged with indignation.

> Your Electoral Grace should not at all think that Luther is dead. Luther will so joyfully rely on that God who has humbled the pope that he will start a game with the Archbishop of Mainz such as few people expect.

The knight addressed a broom in the corner as if it were the archbishop himself:

> Who do you think you are? Have you and the other bishops become nothing but giants and nimrods from Babylon? Why do you hasten like madmen to your own destruction?

There was considerably more to the letter, including a passage in which the writer insisted that he took no joy or pleasure in his

Electoral Grace's shame or dishonor. Perhaps that was true, but Sir Georg seemed almost gleeful as he said, "Tell the captain to have this letter sent immediately. I have given the archbishop exactly fourteen days to change his wicked ways."

The following night the captain and Sir Georg spent a long evening in the gateroom. The knight spoke about troubling news from Wittenberg. He mentioned unrest among the students, conflicts among the churchmen, and confusion among the people.

Sir Georg could not sit still. He paced the room in the chained-bear manner I had seen so often. "How do well-meaning Christians decide which practices to keep and which to abandon? Consider the ways of human nature. Some people cling to the past, even if it is rubble, merely for the sake of tradition. Others clamor to tear down the old church, stone by stone, and build a completely new structure."

Abruptly he turned to face the table. "Captain, I thank you for your patience in dealing with the difficulties of my health and temperament. I ask for your continued patience and understanding. Give me a horse and provisions. I must travel at once to Wittenberg."

For a moment the captain sat in stunned silence. Then he said, *"Bei allen Heiligen*! Have you taken leave of your senses?"

Sir Georg held up his hand. "Hear me out. The situation is desperate. For too long my flock has been left without a shepherd."

Captain von Berlepsch snorted. "The flock is perfectly safe. The shepherd, on the other hand, is a condemned man."

"Hans, please listen. My friends in Wittenberg need to see my face and hear my voice. A brief visit will give them courage to carry on. Melanchthon and Amsdorf and I can plot a safe course for our beloved town. I will make the journey in secret and return at once to my hiding place."

The captain stared at him. "Do you expect me to allow you to risk your life on a fool's errand?"

"If our Lord sees fit to use me as his fool, who are you to deny me?"

The knight strode across the floor and turned smartly to face us, one hand on the hilt of his sword. "You have taught me well, O Lord of Parrots. Look at me now. Do you see any traces of a half-starved monk?"

Sir Georg's full beard was dark and glossy, his hair curled down over his ears, and his cheeks were fuller and ruddier than when I had met him seven months ago.

The captain cursed under his breath.

The knight smiled. "My dear Hans, for so long you have done your duty, looking neither to the right nor to the left. Perhaps God has other plans for you. Look around and ask yourself, 'What is God's will for me?'"

The captain grimaced. "You cannot travel alone, and an armed escort would raise suspicion."

I stepped forward before I realized what I was about to do. "I will accompany him, sir."

"Don't be absurd. Do you think I want both his life and yours upon my head?"

I hesitated only for a moment. "Sir, don't you believe that we are all in the hand of God?"

"Don't be impertinent. You are not my confessor."

"No, sir. But I am no longer an ignorant child." I took a deep breath. "Captain von Berlepsch, I've learned what you taught me. You said my most important duty was to serve Sir Georg, even if it meant risking my life."

Trying to keep my voice steady, I lifted my chin and stared boldly at the captain. "I cannot serve two masters. Lock me up, sir, or I will do all in my power to help Sir Georg escape."

Clearly the captain had not expected resistance from this quarter. He seemed completely at a loss.

Sir Georg said gently, "Hans, my beleaguered friend, I will go to Wittenberg with or without your permission. If I have to leave by lowering myself in a basket, I will do so."

The captain turned to Otto. "You are to keep this blockhead from doing anything regrettable."

The big soldier did not respond.

"Otto? Do I make myself clear?"

Otto shifted his weight and folded his arms across his chest. "Sir, I am your most loyal servant." His voice was very low. "Captain, I beg your pardon for what I am about to say, but if the good *Herr Doktor* asked me to lower him in a basket, I would show him to the gate instead."

Captain von Berlepsch stared at Otto, who stared stubbornly back. The captain looked at me again, and then turned to Sir Georg. "The world has indeed turned upside-down. Martin, I want your word of honor that you will ride directly to Wittenberg, stay no more than two nights, and return at once to the Wartburg."

"Thank you, my dear host, thank you. Seppel and I will be back before you miss us."

The next morning when I took the tray upstairs, Sir Georg was not writing at his desk. The papers that were usually strewn about like autumn leaves were now stacked neatly, anchored by the few volumes that comprised Sir Georg's library. The knight stood at the window wearing his scarlet cloak, his sword at his side.

"Today, Seppel, we eat with our loins girded and shoes on our feet, like the exiled Israelites of old."

We sat down to our meal and gave thanks to God. "Savor the work of good *Frau* Gunda," said the knight. "We shall not dine so well at any crossroads inn."

A short time later, when I led our saddled horses toward the underpass, Captain von Berlepsch was nowhere in sight. I wondered whether, like Pontius Pilate, he had washed his hands of us.

Sir Georg seemed to read my mind. "The captain does not give us his blessing, but neither does he prevent our going."

Otto was alone at the gate. "I pray you will be careful, sir. If any harm were to befall you, it would not go well with the captain."

Suddenly a clear voice called, "Georg, wait!"

Ilse hurried across the courtyard. She was wrapped in her blue cloak, and her hair hung in an untidy braid, as if she had just risen from bed. She stood in front of the knight and pushed back a loose tendril of hair.

"What my father is too proud to tell you, I will say instead. He has served Duke Frederick long and well. If you are captured or killed, Hans von Berlepsch will shoulder the blame."

Sir Georg said gently, "I wish the family von Berlepsch no harm. Do not ask me to forgo this journey."

Ilse drew herself up indignantly. "I ask only that you return safely." She reached out to take his hand. "How I long to ride out of here with you. God speed you, *Herr Doktor*."

For a moment the knight looked as if he might bend to kiss Ilse's hand. Then he made the sign of the cross on her forehead. "God keep you in his grace."

Ilse turned to me, her eyes glistening. "Look after him, Seppel. He needs you more than he will ever know."

CHAPTER 22

The Tale of the Monk

When Sir Georg and I began our journey, the weather was clear and the air was cold and damp. The horses seemed as eager as we to make good time, and they trotted steadily along a well-worn road through the Thuringian Forest. Both the knight and I were considerably better horsemen than when we had first arrived at the Wartburg. Even so, when we stopped to rest the horses at midday, my legs and backside were aching. Sir Georg had long since ceased his cheerful banter about the upcoming reunion with friends.

Often that day I remembered the words of Captain von Berlepsch in the gateroom the night before: "You must do nothing to call attention to yourselves. Do not let him be caught reading or writing in a public place. Never allow him to discuss theology or any other subject unbecoming a knight."

The captain had unrolled a map before me. "I have spoken to Georg of the roads you are to take. During the journey you are never to stay the night within city walls."

"Why is that, sir?"

"Such walls could too easily become a trap. A crossroads inn offers a better chance for flight."

With his finger the captain traced the route from Erfurt through Weimar and Jena. Then the finger moved in a sweeping arc: "You must avoid Leipzig and the surrounding territory, which is ruled by Duke Frederick's cousin, who has sworn to defend the church against the heretic Luther."

At last the captain's finger rested on the word Wittenberg. "You may have to remind your companion that anyone who aids him risks punishment by both church and state."

The captain rolled up the map. "If he is recognized, you too will be questioned. Say only that you are following orders. Your only hope is to appear as ignorant as when you first came to the Wartburg."

"Yes, sir."

Captain von Berlepsch seemed about to say something more. Then he tapped my shoulder lightly with the map. "Go with God, young Burkhardt. That is indeed our best hope."

As Sir Georg and I approached Erfurt, I could see triple spires of a cathedral. The road broadened into a thoroughfare, and soon our horses were tightly hemmed in by lumbering wagons and slow-moving ox carts. When we crossed a wide stone bridge and entered the city gates, the road became a cobbled street. Ahead of us the red-tiled roofs gave way to a huge square, where the cathedral seemed to rise to heaven.

Sir Georg said, "Ah, Seppel, what a joy to be back in Erfurt, one of the dearest places on earth! The university was like a mother to me. To her I owe everything."

I signaled him to stop talking, though none of the students or merchants in the crowded square seemed to be paying attention.

Sir Georg chuckled. "We should drop in to see whether the students are debating the same questions my classmates and I discussed twenty years ago. Every generation of students is convinced that no other generation could have conceived such brilliant ideas."

"Sir, I fear that would be unwise."

The knight sighed. "Do I hear the Lord of Parrots in your voice? Very well, we will forgo the pleasures of the student life."

We stayed the night at an inn outside of Erfurt. After I saw to the horses, I joined Sir Georg at a table. Both of us were so tired that we barely spoke after the serving-woman brought us our meal. The knight and I shared a room with other travelers, but even the raucous snores of a fat merchant did not keep me awake for long.

At daybreak we stood shivering in the innyard as a stableboy led out our horses. Sir Georg groaned as he swung up onto the chestnut. "I am not made for the active life. I much prefer book vellum to saddle leather."

A little distance out of Erfurt we came to a crossroads, and the knight turned his horse into a narrow lane.

"Sir Georg," I said in dismay, "the captain said we were to stay on the main road."

"Allow me one brief excursion. Ride closer that you might better hear the tale." He slowed his horse to a walk, and I drew Tintenfleck up alongside him.

"In the midst of the happy times of which I told you yesterday," said Sir Georg, "I had dark hours from which neither books nor companions could rouse me. During my years at Erfurt it seemed that terrifying emotions roiled under the surface like hidden currents in a river. Such currents are swift and often deadly. Sometimes I would be able to pull myself to shore. Other times I feared that I would be swept helplessly away."

I had to strain to hear the knight's low voice over the steady hoofbeats. "Dear Seppel, how desperately I prayed for guidance. I was a bright young man of one-and-twenty, healthy and well-educated. I had a world of opportunity ahead, yet such dread clutched at my heart. I felt unworthy of the praise heaped on me by instructors and colleagues. I felt shame for accepting my father's generous gifts, even for acknowledging his pride in my accomplishments. I felt overwhelming guilt over countless sins that only God himself could know. For no matter how earnestly I tried, I could never keep his commandments, not even for a single day."

Even as I listened to those heartfelt words, I hoped that this tale would not lead us too far off the main road.

"After I became a master of the liberal arts, my father purchased the books necessary for the study of law." The knight sighed. "How heavily those volumes weighed on me! My first task was to commit to memory the titles of the rules of provincial law. Such an undertaking is not difficult, but how much less gratifying it is to catalog parcels and tracts than to study Scripture or ponder philosophy. However, my father's dearest wish was to see his eldest son an honored magistrate. I was only a few months into my legal studies when he began to take steps to arrange a wealthy marriage for me."

Sir Georg drew his cloak more tightly around him and looked up at the sodden gray sky. "Sixteen years ago on a hot summer night as I walked this very road, a great storm blew across the valley like the wrath of God himself. Half-deafened by the thunder, whipped by the wind, I fell to my knees in terror. A bolt of lightning struck so near

I could smell burning sulfur. I cried out words I had known since childhood: 'Saint Anne, save me!' With fear prickling my nostrils, I added, 'I swear I will become a monk!'"

Then the knight was silent for so long that I could not tell whether he had ended the conversation or was waiting for me to respond. At last I ventured softly, "And so you became a monk."

"How my friends wept when the gate of the monastery swung shut behind me! How very angry and disappointed my father was to have his dream shattered!" Sir Georg smiled wryly. "He had no qualms about telling me so when he attended my ordination two years later. This was our first meeting since I had entered the cloister. As we sat together at the dinner for which he had generously paid, I spoke of the sign from God that had led me to the monastery. My father said, 'Let us hope that it was not an illusion and a deception.' And then he said, 'Have you not also heard that parents are to be obeyed?' Those bitter words have remained with me all these years."

For a little while the dull thud of hooves was the only sound, and then the knight continued, his voice stronger now. "During my exile at the Wartburg I have come to realize the truth of what my father said that day. I was wrong to make that vow. I know now that Satan does indeed entrap those who become priests and monks and nuns in a vain attempt to enhance their standing with God. For we cannot by our own reason or strength come to him, Seppel, no matter what vows we make or how many prayers we offer."

Sir Georg stared out across the valley. "Yet it was God's will that I learn the wisdom of the schools and experience the sanctity of the monastery. When I criticize the practices of the church, my enemies cannot claim that I condemn something about which I know nothing."

We rode on in silence until we reached the main road once more.

Sir Georg patted the sword which hung at his side. "I am subject neither to bishop nor duke, neither pope nor emperor. In the service of a greater Master, my weapon is the sword of the Spirit, which is the Word of God."

CHAPTER 23

At the Crossroads

During that secret journey in the company of Germany's most famous outlaw, I felt grateful to be the confidant of this extraordinary man. Yet I found myself uneasy with the notion that a man of God could renounce his vows so decisively. What if all the monks and nuns in Germany were to leave the cloisters? What would become of the monasteries and the convents?

If those who had dedicated their lives to God became no different from the rest of us, then who would carry on the work of the church? When my mind was not lulled by the rhythm of hoofbeats and the creak of saddle-leather, such thoughts continued to trouble me on the road to Wittenberg.

The knight's lack of caution continued to trouble me as well. One evening after I saw to the horses and entered a village inn, I heard him say to another guest, "Then it is true that the Archbishop of Mainz persists in his folly. Has he no conscience? Has he no shame?"

Hastily I stepped forward. "Sir Georg, have you ordered a meal, or shall I speak to the innkeeper?"

He ignored the question. "Do you hear, Seppel, what this man has told me? At Halle, the Archbishop of Mainz continues to permit trafficking in indulgences. Is his Electoral Grace a bishop or a wolf?"

The other guest guffawed. He appeared to be deep in drink, and he signaled the innkeeper for another round.

I glowered at Sir Georg.

The knight acknowledged my expression with a sigh. He said to his table companion, "You seem to be well-informed in certain matters. Tell me, if you please, the merits of the local brewery."

The next night I patted Tintenfleck's muzzle and stepped out of the stable of another crossroads inn. Tall torches ringed the dark yard, and softly falling snow made each flame into a glowing orb.

"I know you," said a familiar voice behind me.

I turned in surprise. In the doorway of the stable stood a young nobleman, a stranger to me.

"Actually," he continued, "I know that black horse. I wouldn't have remembered you except for Tintenfleck. Your own face is quite common."

The slighting tone triggered my recognition. Before me stood Erich, the squire who had accompanied Sir Gottfried on my journey from Spalt. He was taller than he had been seven months ago, and traces of dark stubble adorned his chin.

None of the captain's warnings had prepared me for such an encounter. Was Erich a friend or a foe? Should I acknowledge that I knew him?

Before I could decide how to respond, Erich took a step closer. "Why are you dressed in such clothing? You're no page." His voice was unmistakably hostile.

Drawing myself up stiffly, I said, "You are mistaken. We have never met."

I turned and strode away with what I hoped was confidence.

Behind my back I heard him, louder now. "What's your game, peasant?"

My breath quickened in the cold air. What could I say? What should I do? Several travelers were standing in the yard. They looked up with interest at the squire's words.

Erich called to me again. "Who are you, pretender? What right have you to strut about with a sword?" His words were clearly intended for the onlookers to hear.

I felt a burning cold ache begin somewhere deep inside, and I was afraid I might stop breathing altogether.

From behind me came the final taunt. "If you are a false page, then your master must be a false knight!"

Instinctively I drew my sword and turned to face him. "How dare you accuse my master?"

Grinning, the squire unsheathed his own sword. The onlookers murmured and nudged one another. I hoped that one of them would order us to put down our weapons. With dismay I realized that they were all commoners. None of them would dare to interfere with the actions of the nobility.

"I—I do not wish to fight," I said.

"Then you're not only a peasant but also a coward."

"I am no coward," I said through gritted teeth. My sword arm trembled slightly, whether in fear or rage I could not tell.

Erich glanced around him, clearly enjoying the spectacle. He took a few steps left, then right, and each time I turned to face him. A moment later we were circling like wary dogs.

Again he flung the words like a gauntlet. "Is your master as great a pretender as you are?"

I swung my sword so suddenly that the squire barely had time to parry. The clanging of our blades startled me so that I did not think to press my advantage.

At once the squire was back in his stance, sword at the ready. "You won't be so lucky again."

There was no help for it. I tried to remember all the advice the captain had given me, but in that snow-trampled yard, as the squire and I circled one another, our breath visible in the cold night air, I could remember only the green parrot's rasping cry: *Was sehrt, das lehrt! Was sehrt, das lehrt!*

Again I lunged toward the mocking face, and this time my sword met empty air. Then Erich lunged, and I parried him neatly. At his next thrust my blade countered his, but my boots slipped, and I nearly staggered.

"Balance is all!" hissed the captain's voice in my head.

I was failing the captain miserably—and failing Sir Georg and Ilse and all the household of the Wartburg. I could not allow the ring of curious onlookers to know that I was indeed a pretender. Grimly I faced the squire.

A moment later I rushed him and laid on such a rain of blows that he was hard pressed to defend himself. The ringing blades echoed across the yard. In my fury I grew careless, and my opponent's blade scratched my left arm.

He pulled back, as did I, both of us panting.

Erich sneered. "Admit that I have shed the blood of a pretender, and I'll do you no further harm."

I glanced at my bleeding arm. Erich was taller and stronger than I. His reach was longer, and he had a lifetime of practice over my few months. In such a situation, what would the captain do?

Beyond our raised blades, I could already read triumph in the squire's eyes. I allowed uncertainty to show in my face. Steadying my sword arm, I whispered, "I am no pretender."

I tried not to think about the spectators, tried not to think about anything but my grueling hours of practice. Long ago in the armory the captain had traced a cross over my tunic with the point of his sword. I heard his voice: "The four openings. Of course, the spot you aim for in your opponent is the one you protect most fiercely in yourself."

Smugly the squire advanced as I retreated, my steps uneven, my breath ragged. My parries of his hard sure strokes were weak. All the time I concentrated on that invisible cross on my opponent's tunic, watched and waited for the moment I knew would come.

My boots seemed far more slippery than Erich's, and when I nearly lost my footing, the squire pressed in, his sword sweeping grandly for the benefit of the spectators. Deftly I lunged, and my well-measured thrust found its mark. With a yelp the squire drew back, and just then a deep voice rang across the yard.

"Halt! I order you to stop at once!"

Without taking my eyes off my opponent, I prepared to relax my sword. As soon as Erich saw me straighten from my fighting stance, he lowered his own sword. With a contemptuous snort he sheathed his weapon.

A grizzled knight strode over the trampled snow, and I saw the rugged face of Sir Gottfried.

He looked from one to the other of us. "What stupid game are you two playing?"

"Don't you know him?" said the squire. "This is the peasant boy from Franconia!"

The grizzled knight's eyes flickered over me with no sign of recognition. He turned back to the squire. "No peasant handles a sword like that. You must beg his pardon for your error."

When Erich opened his mouth to protest, Sir Gottfried added, "He drew blood, did he not? Erich, are you telling me a commoner could hold his own against you?"

Only then did I see the dark stain on the squire's torn tunic.

The next morning I was in the stable before sunrise. The cut on my arm ached, and I had not slept well. Sir Georg and I had agreed to be on the road at first light. I led the saddled horses out into the yard.

Sir Gottfried stood beside the stable door. "It seems you were not destined to carry a broom after all."

I grinned, then caught myself and tried to pretend confusion.

Sir Gottfried smiled. "I do not concern myself with the mysterious workings of the Saxon court. I know only that the Lord of Parrots must have taught you well." He reached out to touch my shoulder. "Go with God, young swordsman."

CHAPTER 24

Among Friends

I did not feel like a swordsman. Would a true swordsman become sickened by imagining how differently the fight might have ended? As Sir Georg and I rode steadily onward, my arm ached. The knight did not notice my discomfort. He spent the afternoon whistling cheerfully whenever he was not telling stories about his friends in Wittenberg.

Earlier he and I had agreed that when we reached our destination, we would never mention our hiding place or those who sheltered us. The closer our horses brought us to Wittenberg, the less real the Wartburg seemed, as if the world the knight and I shared had never existed at all.

"Look there," said Sir Georg, gesturing into the gray twilight. "Wittenberg lies just ahead."

I strained my eyes to catch sight of spires and towers and saw only the faintest outline of buildings above the trees on the horizon. My companion urged his tired horse to move faster. Reluctantly I nudged Tintenfleck into a trot.

Long before we entered the gate, I could see that Wittenberg was considerably smaller than Erfurt. The double set of walls that fortified the town was bounded by a river, and the air was permeated by a swampish reek and the raw smells of the market. When we rode into town, Sir Georg pointed out the Castle Church near the gate and the Town Church on the market square. "And there is Cranach House, home of my dear friend Lucas Cranach. Just down the street is the shop of Christian Doerring, the goldsmith."

At the other end of town Sir Georg showed me the grounds of the college and then halted in front of a small house. He dismounted, tossed me the reins, and walked quickly up the path. He rapped on the door, then turned and grinned at me. I did not smile back.

The door opened, and a young housewife in a white cap and apron peered out at him.

Sir Georg swept her a courtly bow. "Good *Frau* Melanchthon, is the professor at home?"

"I beg your pardon, sir, but Master Melanchthon may not be disturbed."

Sir Georg put a hand on the hilt of his sword. "'May not be disturbed?' Do you presume to tell a knight that a commoner 'may not be disturbed'?"

The young woman reddened. "My husband has many responsibilities, sir. In the evening he needs time for his studies."

Sir Georg relaxed his stance. "You are a good wife to him. Ask him, if you please, whether he will greet a visitor from the Kingdom of the Birds."

Frau Melanchthon sighed. "Yet another Greek riddle? Very well, sir. I will ask him." The door closed.

Sir Georg signaled me to tie up the horses and join him on the doorstep. "The Wittenbergers know what a gem they have in their professor of Greek. They married Philip to the mayor's daughter not long after he arrived."

Abruptly the door was flung wide to reveal a slender young man, fashionably dressed except for sleeves rolled up past the elbow and a dark smudge of ink alongside his nose. After stepping over the threshold to peer at Sir Georg, he gasped and reached out both arms to embrace the knight.

Sir Georg clasped his friend heartily. Over the professor's shoulder he said to the housewife, "My dear, I kissed you on your wedding day. Do you not know your husband's friend, Luther?"

"Martin Luther! How can it be?" *Frau* Melanchthon's surprise changed to panic. "What do you mean, walking about so boldly? Get inside!" Urgently she tugged at the sleeves of the two men. I managed to slip inside before she closed the door.

"Martin," she hissed, "are you mad? What are you doing here?"

Master Melanchthon put his arm around his wife. "I assume he is hoping to be made welcome." His voice was gentle, and he had an air of earnest good will.

Frau Melanchthon threw up her hands. "*Ach*, Philip! Of course Martin is welcome here, but I don't want the whole town in after him."

Sir Georg said, "My young friend is Seppel Burkhardt. His uncle Spalatin has provided me with a curbing rein, you see."

Frau Melanchthon said pertly, "Spalatin is a very wise man."

After dinner Sir Georg and Master Melanchthon had a long conversation, some of it in German, some in Latin, with occasional phrases that might have been Greek. The two men hardly noticed when *Frau* Melanchthon and I retired to the kitchen, where we listened to the rise and fall of their voices, one impassioned and the other soothing.

Frau Melanchthon said, "They are like fire and water. How good it is for Philip to have dear Martin here." She smiled. "And how comical it is to hear you call him Sir Georg."

Her light remark reminded me that the man I served belonged to the world beyond the Wartburg. Here his friends called him by his true name. They knew the real man while I knew only his shadow, my make-believe knight. Erich's spiteful words echoed in my head. I was indeed a false page, and my master was a false knight. I had fought to protect him, but no blade could protect me from the stinging truth of the squire's words.

The following morning when Master Melanchthon went off to his lecture, Sir Georg led me to a dark little shop near the market square. Finely wrought rings lay in a glass-topped case. Links of chain gleamed under the circle of lamplight where a portly bespectacled man set down his tools and stood to greet us.

"I wish to buy a gold chain," said Sir Georg. He pointed to the table at which the goldsmith had been working. "I will have that one."

"But I've hardly begun it, sir. Let me show you another nearly the same."

Sir Georg frowned. "I have made my choice. Do you refuse me?"

The goldsmith's face showed irritation, but his words were polite. "Oh, no, sir. I merely suggest that you might consider another."

"I cannot wait. I will take that chain exactly as it is."

"But, sir, such a length is completely useless!"

Sir Georg drew himself up proudly. "Do you dare to question me? Do you not know who I am?"

The goldsmith seemed about to answer sharply but thought better of it. "No, sir, I do not."

Sir Georg turned toward the door. "Christian Doerring, my time in Wittenberg is more precious than your gold. Perhaps Lucas Cranach will be more gracious to his old friend Luther."

He began to walk out the door as the goldsmith sputtered, "Luther? Martin, wait! Is that really you?"

The two men embraced, and then the goldsmith wiped his spectacles with a cloth and chuckled. "You had me fairly, Martin. You caught me out indeed!"

He was so delighted by Sir Georg's prank that he locked up his shop and accompanied us to Cranach House. At the door a servant greeted the goldsmith by name.

Herr Doerring gestured toward Sir Georg and told the servant, "My noble companion is a man of some renown. Send for your master at once."

The servant led us into a small chamber. A few moments later, a ruddy-cheeked man with a black mustache and keen dark eyes entered the room. "Good morning, Christian," *Herr* Cranach said to the goldsmith. To Sir Georg he said, "I welcome you, noble sir. How may I be of service?"

Sir Georg said, "I wish to have my portrait painted."

"Very good, sir. We must arrange a sitting for you." The painter eyed the knight appraisingly, and suddenly one black eyebrow shot up. He signaled the servant to leave the room.

When the door closed, *Herr* Cranach crossed his arms. "I beg your pardon, sir, but it is quite impossible for me to paint you."

Sir Georg frowned. "What do you mean—impossible? Do you not know who I am?"

"I regret to inform you, sir, that I cannot risk spoiling my canvas with such a face."

Sir Georg recoiled in surprise. The goldsmith and I gaped at the painter.

Cranach bowed. "Now, if you will excuse me, Doctor Luther, I must return to my work."

After a moment of stunned silence, Sir Georg threw back his head and laughed.

The goldsmith shook his head. "Lucas, however did you see through him?"

"I am an artist, Christian. Such is my business." Cranach clapped Sir Georg on the back. "Welcome home, Martin. Will you allow me to paint your portrait after all?"

During the hours of Sir Georg's formal sitting, several professors from the university visited the chamber where the painter stood at his easel. While Cranach worked, Sir Georg and the visitors discussed recent disturbances in the town, including riots in which church statues and stained-glass windows had been broken.

Cranach said, "Stop scowling, Martin. Try to look as if your mind is on things above."

He glanced toward the stool where I sat trying to keep from fidgeting. Signaling to the curly-haired boy who fetched the brushes, Cranach said, "Luke, show Sir Georg's page around the shop."

The boy grinned. "Yes, Father."

I followed Luke into a well-lighted room where a dozen men, old and young, stood at easels or sat at long tables. The odor of paints and other substances made my eyes water.

The boy inhaled deeply and sighed with pleasure. "This is our workshop," he said. He led me from easel to easel, remarking on each work in progress:

"Those women are undressed because they are goddesses."

"We can't finish the Blessed Virgin's cloak till the next shipment of azurite arrives."

"See that corner of sky? That's my own work."

At one table a man sat making a series of cuts into a pen-and-ink drawing on a wooden block. The blockcutter handled his blade as easily as if he were slicing a pear, his smooth strokes following the lines of ink precisely. I watched him use the point of the knife to lift the tiny slivers of wood. A small pile of the delicate cuttings lay beside the block.

Luke whispered, "It will take him days to cut away the spaces so that only the ink of the drawing remains. Then Father will send the woodcut to the printer."

The blockcutter looked at me, his eyes as blue as a painted sky. "If I do my work well, that picture will appear in a hundred books, maybe more."

His words made me painfully aware that I had no workshop, no skills, no corner of sky to call my own.

That evening when Sir Georg and Master Melanchthon and I met in the home of Doctor Amsdorf, the knight said to his friends, "I am disappointed that neither of you responded to my treatise on monastic vows. When can I expect to see those pages in print?"

His companions seemed puzzled. When Sir Georg questioned them further, he learned that they had not received any of the writing he had recently sent by way of Spalatin. Master Melanchthon said that the documents might have been lost or misplaced. Doctor Amsdorf suggested that the messenger might have been waylaid.

Sir Georg frowned. "Such news would disturb me less than to learn that Spalatin, whom I have trusted in all things, has betrayed me."

He turned to me. "I beg your pardon, Seppel, for speaking uncharitably of your uncle. Yet what a bitter drop to find in the sweet company of friends."

He sat down heavily at Doctor Amsdorf's desk. "Get me paper and ink, Nicholas. I will write to him at once."

Master Melanchthon said, "Spalatin must have a reason for withholding your work. He is responsible to the elector and must be mindful of the political weather. Before he sets sail, he must wait to see whether the wind is favorable."

Sir Georg snorted. "Wind or no wind, Spalatin is rowing against the current."

He bent over the desk, and the only sound in the room was the furious scratching of his pen. Once he looked up to say, "Philip, as it is clear that I cannot rely on Spalatin, I shall leave letters here for you to deliver."

The harshness of his voice made me burn with anger and shame.

Again the knight looked up, brandishing his pen like a weapon. "How can Spalatin be so misguided as to keep timely words from people who need desperately to read them?"

Master Melanchthon said gently, "Martin, it may be that the people are in more desperate need of—well, of timeless words." He turned to Doctor Amsdorf. "Do you remember, Nicholas, what happens every time we discuss the need for a better German translation of the New Testament?"

Doctor Amsdorf nodded. "Our duties prevent us from taking on such an endeavor." He leaned toward Sir Georg. "Tell me, Martin, what are your duties these days?"

When the knight did not respond, Master Melanchthon said, "Neither Spalatin nor the elector could object to your translating the Holy Scriptures. God has blessed you with keen understanding, a poet's tongue, and now this rare gift of solitude."

Sir Georg looked from one friend to the other. He shook his head slowly. "Philip, I lack your skill in Greek. Such an undertaking would be impossible without you beside me." His face brightened suddenly. "I will find myself a hiding place in Wittenberg. Only my closest friends will know where I am, and we need not trouble Spalatin with the details of our plan."

I rose to my feet and glared at him. "My uncle is trying to protect you from—from yourself, sir. Do you have so few enemies that you can afford to include your friends among them?" My words tumbled out faster and faster. "Do you have so many friends that you can afford to endanger any of them? *Frau* Melanchthon says she's already heard rumors about your presence here. You can't possibly be so foolish as to think you could hide in Wittenberg."

The three men stared at me in astonishment.

Doggedly I continued. "Think about the captain. Think about Ilse! You promised that you would return to the Wartburg."

I stopped, mouth open, horrified to realize what I had just done.

CHAPTER 25

Of Ink and Candlewax

In the silence that followed my outburst, the three men did not look at one another. What agony of mind I felt as I stood before them. My careless words had put at risk not only Sir Georg and the household of the Wartburg but also these friends in Wittenberg.

Doctor Amsdorf was the first to speak. Leaning forward in his chair, he said, "Martin, I believe I met your captain one night in the Thuringian Forest. He was rather unpleasant to me, and he bruised our poor driver. I prefer not to dwell on that event."

Sir Georg said briskly, "Then let us put an end to this discussion."

He and the others were silent again.

I tried to think of something to say.

At last Sir Georg sighed heavily. "Philip, I should like to borrow a Greek grammar. I ought to consult an Erasmus text as well. Would you ask Spalatin to send those to me?"

Slowly the knight turned toward the desk and picked up the quill, murmuring, "I must add a postscript to my letter."

Doctor Amsdorf and Master Melanchthon and I listened once more to the scratching of the pen in the quiet room.

Then Sir Georg turned to face us again. "Philip, please ask your good wife to pack provisions for our journey tomorrow."

Early the following morning we made our farewells to the Melanchthons. On the way out of Wittenberg, Sir Georg did not stop at Cranach House or the goldsmith's shop. He kept the horses at a brisk trot for several miles beyond the town gate. When he finally reined in the chestnut, he did not turn in the saddle, as I did, to gaze down the path we had come.

"I have put my hand to the plow, Seppel, and I will not look back."

I took a deep breath. "Sir, I was wrong to upbraid you last night and unbelievably stupid to speak of our hiding place."

The knight smiled. "*Ach*, Seppel, when the heart is full, the mouth overflows. I was wrong to slander those who care for me. Let us forgive one another and move onward, for we have a long road ahead."

We made good time on the way back to the Wartburg. The weather remained clear, and snow sparkled on the trees and rooftops. Sir Georg was not inclined to linger in the towns through which we passed. He spoke little, but when I rode alongside him, I saw that his lips were often moving.

On the final day of our journey, Sir Georg and I caught sight of the snow-capped towers of the Wartburg. I urged our tired horses onward, wondering how soon I might see friendly faces inside the castle walls.

At last we began the steep ascent that led to the castle, dismounting so that our boot prints joined the tracks of donkeys in the snow. We rounded a bend in the winding path and saw the drawbridge up ahead. Framed in the window above the castle gate was the figure of Ilse.

"Look, sir!" I pointed to the window, and Sir Georg raised a hand in greeting. Ilse waved and then disappeared from sight.

Panting to keep up with Tintenfleck, who clearly understood that he was almost home, I said, "Do you think she has been watching for us every day?"

Sir Georg chuckled. "No doubt her father has had news of our approach."

The smaller door within the great door opened wide, and Otto stepped out to greet us. "How glad I am to see you, sir!" he said, taking the reins from Sir Georg.

One of Otto's strong arms swept around my shoulders and clasped me in a quick embrace. "*Willkommen*, Seppel! How good to have you back again."

Otto had hardly let me go when I was enveloped by Hermina, who kissed me soundly and then stood at arm's length to look me up and down. "What a dull time it has been without you, Seppel. I have had only this great lout for company." She ducked to avoid Otto's playful swipe.

Then Otto became formal once again. "The captain is waiting to see both of you."

When we entered the gateroom, Master Klüglein squawked a greeting and sidled along his perch.

Captain von Berlepsch stood at the window. "Welcome back, Georg. I trust you had a pleasant visit."

"Very pleasant, Captain, but altogether too brief. I shall return to Wittenberg when I have completed my next project. By Easter, I should think."

"Indeed," said the captain drily. "Have you informed his Grace, the Elector, of your plan?"

"It matters not what the world thinks." Sir Georg began to pace the room, speaking with great animation. "I will need good quality paper, the best ink, and perhaps a dozen new quills. Also a sizable supply of candles. If you please, Captain, I prefer not to be disturbed for meals. I will send Seppel to the kitchen when I require sustenance."

The captain raised an eyebrow. "I'm sure Gunda will be delighted to hear that. Will there be anything else?"

"Yes. Plenty of firewood in my chamber. I cannot write if my fingers are aching with cold. And now, Captain, if you will excuse me, I must begin my work."

He left the room without waiting for a reply.

The captain looked at me. "What is he up to now?"

"He intends to translate the New Testament, sir."

"By Easter?" The captain snorted. "Is it the ink or the candlewax that makes a scribbler mad?" He eyed me critically. "See that you rid yourself of the stench of the road before you join my family for the evening meal."

Until that night I had never sat to dine with the family von Berlepsch. When I entered the dining hall, Captain von Berlepsch and the three noblewomen were already seated. I bowed, and the captain gestured toward a chair.

Lady von Berlepsch looked thinner and paler than ever. Even by candlelight, blue veins were visible under her tightly drawn skin, and her cheekbones jutted out sharply under dark-hollowed eyes. Beside her, Dame Adela sat with her usual air of disapproval. Ilse wore a fur-trimmed gown, and light flickered over gold netting in her hair. Her lips were slightly parted, and though she said nothing, she seemed about to smile. With a start I realized that she was glad to see me.

The captain gave thanks to God, and Hermina brought in the first course. Lady von Berlepsch turned to me. "Now we must hear all about your journey to Wittenberg."

That evening I forgot that I was not born to sit among the nobility. Even Dame Adela smiled at my telling of the goldsmith whom Sir Georg could fool and the painter whom he could not.

But when I reported that the knight had sat for a portrait, the captain said, "*Bei allen Heiligen*! Where is this portrait now? Hanging in the Castle Church?"

Why had it not occurred to me that the existence of that painting was a risk?

The captain muttered to himself, but Lady von Berlepsch said, "The good doctor has returned safely. Let us hope that his new writing project will keep him from becoming restless again."

Dame Adela frowned. "Have we not German Bibles already? Why does he waste his time?"

She was looking at me, so I ventured a response. "Sir Georg says his translation will embrace the German language. He wants to shape the lines the way that people speak in their homes or in the market square."

"In the market square?" said Dame Adela. "Among those too ignorant to read at all? They have priests to interpret the Bible for them."

I was reluctant to contradict her, but I felt obliged to defend the knight. "Sir Georg says the Scriptures ought to be in every home. He says everyone should know the Gospel and be able to share it with others."

Dame Adela sniffed. "Would he have the Word of God become as common as a tale told in a kitchen? What if peasants began discussing the Scriptures? What if tradesmen were to decide they know as much as the priests—or the nobility?"

Lady von Berlepsch said softly, "I fear that without proper guidance the common people will misunderstand the Scriptures. They will take wrong actions and rebel against the authorities. Surely breaking church windows and beating priests is not pleasing to God."

Captain von Berlepsch said, "Our friend the scribbler has often reminded me that the Word of God is sharper than a two-edged sword. Let him who wields it be wary of the blade."

Ilse looked slyly at me. "As we are speaking of swords, I should mention that we had a visitor while you were away. Sir Gottfried told us that he met you at an inn. Is your arm healing well?"

"Yes, *Fräulein*." I could not tell whether or not she was truly sympathetic.

"Good." A smile played about Ilse's mouth. "That Erich is so conceited. I'm glad you stuck him."

"Ilse!" cried Lady von Berlepsch.

Dame Adela crossed herself, but Captain von Berlepsch caught my eye. Ever so slightly, he raised his tankard.

During the first week after our return, Sir Georg worked almost without ceasing. I filled his inkwell, sharpened his quills, and tended the fire in the stove. The knight kept such long hours that I spent few nights in my own bedchamber. Instead I dozed on a pallet on the floor near the stove, waking up chilled when the fire burned down to embers.

Although my lord no longer made any attempt to play the part of a knight, I became an exemplary page, performing my duties so well that the rhythm of his work was never disturbed.

One evening, Sir Georg sighed over the scratched-out lines that covered his paper. "Here, Seppel, you have a neat hand. Copy this, if you please, or the printer will not be able to make head or tail of it."

He ran a hand through his hair, a habit so strong that the dark curls at his temples stood nearly on end. More than ever before, he looked the part of a prisoner, one writing frantically and ceaselessly in hopes of securing his own release. I had no doubt that Sir Georg would indeed leave the Wartburg as soon as he finished his translation.

I knelt to stir the glowing embers, then wiped the soot from my hands and approached the table. Sir Georg set a clean sheet before me and placed his heavily inked translation at my left.

I dipped the quill into the inkwell, carefully read the corrected lines, and began copying the words as neatly as I could. A passage from the Gospel of Matthew was my first contribution to Sir Georg's project:

Look at the birds of the air: they neither sow nor reap nor gather into barns, and yet your heavenly Father feeds them. Are you not of more value than they?

In the days that followed, Sir Georg set me the task of making a fair copy whenever his manuscript was thoroughly marked with corrections or when exhaustion had made his handwriting nearly illegible.

At such times he often went directly to his bed, where he fell almost instantly asleep. Other times he sat before the stove, crossing his arms, closing his eyes, and resting his chin upon his chest. As happened so often, I could not tell whether his attitude was one of sleep or prayer. I do know that he seemed to draw comfort from the scratching of my quill, evidence that the work progressed.

One morning when I woke in the gray light of dawn, Sir Georg was not at his table or in the little sleeping chamber. I rose from the pallet and wondered whether to stir up the fire. Yawning, I pulled on my tunic and wool doublet, slipped into my boots, and went in search of my knight.

I found him in the kitchen, sitting on a stool beside the table where Gunda stood, white to the elbows with flour. A dusting of flour lay like new-fallen snow over the knight's head and shoulders. Nearby, Dolf was chopping onions, red-eyed but utterly attentive to the knight's words.

"Imagine what would happen," Sir Georg said, "if good *Frau* Gunda merely mixed the flour into a paste and shoved it straight into the oven. Of course, she would never do that. Look at her working the dough, kneading it with her fine strong hands, turning it over and over. So it is with the daily bread of the soul. Whenever we hear the Scriptures, we are to ponder the words, turning them over and over in our minds. The more thoroughly we work the Word of God, the more it satisfies and nourishes our lives."

One afternoon when I was flexing my aching wrist, I heard light footsteps and a quick rapping at the door. Ilse stood in the drafty corridor, clutching her arms under her sleeves.

Sir Georg looked up and smiled. "Come in and warm yourself, my dear."

Ilse stepped over the threshold, her gown trailing behind her, and pulled the door shut before she moved toward the glowing stove. Abruptly she said to the knight, "I wish to help you in any way I can. What would you have me do?"

Sir Georg did not seem at all surprised. "It is fitting that we look for ways to serve God. *Fräulein*, ask your father whether you and Seppel might ride in the forest today. My faithful page has been too long at his task."

"No," said Ilse. "I do not wish to go. I want to help you in your work."

CHAPTER 26

The Word Like Fire

Ilse repeated, "*Herr Doktor*, tell me what I can do to help."

Sir Georg seemed to study the paper in his hands. He sat silent for so long that I wondered whether he had forgotten her presence. Certainly I had not. There she stood, beautiful and stubborn and proud, in the room which no other woman of the Wartburg had yet entered.

At last Sir Georg held out a sheaf of pages. "Take these to the kitchen and read them to *Frau* Gunda. Tell me what she thinks of them."

Ilse stared at him. "You would have me run messages for the cook?"

"*Fräulein*, do you not remember that the Apostle Paul tells us that—"

Ilse snatched the papers, turned abruptly, and left the room, slamming the door behind her.

I gaped at the knight. "Sir, why did you tell her to do that?"

"What does the Apostle Paul write in his marvelous letter to the Galatians? 'Let him that is taught in the word share with him that teacheth in all good things.' And a few lines later, 'remember, we are reminded that we ought to do good to all, especially to those who are of the household of faith.'" Sir Georg smiled and picked up his quill. "What a blessing that Ilse is eager to share the Gospel with others!"

"Yes, sir," I said, but I was not quite convinced.

We were engrossed once more in our work when heavy footsteps in the corridor were followed by the thump of a fist on the door. Sir Georg called out a greeting, and the door swung open to reveal Gunda, red-faced from exertion.

"Good day, dear *Frau*," said the knight, rising immediately. "What brings you here?"

The cook crossed her arms over her broad chest. "Why did you send that meddlesome child to my kitchen? She is as full of drivel as a pig's bladder! She claims that everyone who takes the Sacrament ought to receive both bread and wine. "

Then came a flurry of steps down the corridor, and Ilse pushed her way past the cook, still clutching the sheaf of pages. "*Herr Doktor,* did you hear her say that the Word of God is drivel?"

The cook snorted. "Foolish girl, are you a priest that I should listen to you? I will listen to him—" she jerked her chin toward the knight— "but never to you."

Ilse glared at the cook. "Armed with the Scriptures, we are all priests, you ignorant woman. The people of God are themselves a priesthood." She turned to Sir Georg. "Isn't that so?"

"Do you hear her, *Herr Doktor*?" said the cook. "She is quite mad."

Ilse gasped. "How dare you speak to me that way?"

Sir Georg held up his hands. "Dear Christian friends, is this the way our Lord calls us to serve one another?"

Gunda shrugged. "I am called to the kitchen, and I will let no fool keep me from that calling." She stared pointedly at Ilse, then turned and left the room, slamming the door behind her.

Ilse brandished the rolled pages like a weapon. "Why didn't you tell that stupid peasant that what I said was true? I read the words straight from the Scriptures. Still she would not believe."

The knight said gently, "Ilse, do you remember what the Apostle Paul tells us are the fruits of the Spirit?"

Ilse said through gritted teeth, "The fruits of the Spirit are love, joy, peace, patience, gentleness, goodness, faith, and temperance."

"Indeed. Those words were addressed to a congregation in which there was great discord, for Paul wrote to the Galatians, 'But when you bite and snap at one another, take heed that you do not eat each other up!'"

Ilse stamped her foot. "But blind ignorance must be confronted! How can the church be reformed if people refuse to accept the truth?"

"My zealous young friend, let us begin by clarifying the difference between Law and Gospel. The lawgiver Moses threatened and rebuked his people, but in the Gospel our Lord Jesus invites us kindly. Jesus the shepherd leads his flock instead of driving them forth before Him. The people of the church must be coaxed down this new path. Too sudden a change in their accustomed ways would scatter them as surely as would a pack of wolves."

Sir Georg gazed into the flames of the stove. "I cannot help but think of the words of the prophet Jeremiah in which the Lord says, 'Is not my Word like fire, and like a hammer that breaks the stone?'"

He sighed. "Far too many people glorify the breaking. In their zeal they give little thought to the rebuilding that must come after."

Ilse sniffed. "Your favorite apostle also writes that when men build on the foundation of Jesus Christ, the fire must test what sort of work each one has done."

"You are perhaps too adept a pupil, my dear."

A few evenings later there came quick steps in the corridor and a timid rap at Sir Georg's door. Hermina entered, dropped a hasty curtsey, and began speaking at once. "Oh, sir, the soldiers are saying things that can't possibly be true."

The knight set down his quill. "What do they say that troubles you?"

"Otto told me that they say that one need not do good works. The soldiers say that one who has faith in Christ Jesus is free to commit any kind of sin. They say they read it themselves in the Scriptures."

"Come and sit here by the stove, my dear." Sir Georg pulled his chair closer to the fire and sat on the stool beside her.

"Tell me, does Otto love you?"

Hermina put a hand to her cheek. "Oh, sir, what a question!"

"Does he love you, Hermina?"

"He—he tells me so." She ducked her head to hide her face.

"Do you love him?"

She lifted her head. "With all my heart."

"And if you sinned against Otto—if you hurt him, would he forgive you?"

"But I would never do such a thing!"

"Why not?"

"I wish him only the best, sir. I want him to be safe and well. I want him to be at peace."

"Would you do everything within your power to keep him safe and well and at peace?"

"Indeed I would!"

Sir Georg said, "And if human love is so powerful, how much greater must be the love of our Lord for his people. He gave us no other commandment but to love one another. If we truly have faith in him, we wish to follow his example. We cannot help but break out into good works."

He smiled. "My dear, real faith does not question whether good works are to be done." He nodded toward the glowing stove. "Why, it is as impossible to separate works from faith as to separate heat and light from fire."

The next day there came a frenzy of knocking at the door, and Hermina appeared once more. "I do beg your pardon, *Herr Doktor,* but Lady von Berlepsch wishes to see you!"

Sir Georg waved his quill with an air of mild protest. "I will call on her as soon as I finish this page."

"Oh no, sir!" Hermina fairly squeaked. "She and Dame Adela are on their way to your chamber." She glanced around the room. "Stir up the fire at once, Seppel. You can't expect her ladyship to sit in the cold."

The knight set down his quill and watched with amusement as Hermina picked up his rumpled cloak and draped it over a chair, then hung his sword belt on a hook in the wall. But when Hermina approached the paper strewn about on the floor, he said firmly, "Leave those pages where they are. They are intended to be seen and read, not hidden away."

Hermina looked as if she wished she could tidy up Sir Georg as well. His tunic was wrinkled and his hair was standing on end, for he had snatched only a few fitful hours of sleep before returning to his task.

We heard footsteps in the corridor, and two servants appeared, one carrying chairs and the other a set of embroidered cushions. The men bowed to the knight and then crossed the small room to set the chairs directly before the stove, where flames were snapping eagerly at the new kindling.

The servants bowed again and silently withdrew. Then came quiet footsteps, slow and deliberate. Clad in fur-lined cloaks, the two noblewomen appeared in the doorway, Lady von Berlepsch leaning against the arm of Dame Adela.

Sir Georg stepped forward to offer his arm to the lady. She smiled and loosened her grip from the other woman, whose face looked as disagreeable as ever.

The knight helped Lady von Berlepsch to a chair and arranged the cushions to her satisfaction. Dame Adela took the other chair, brushing off Hermina's attempts to assist her.

"Thank you, Hermina," said Lady von Berlepsch. "You may go." The maid curtseyed and left the room, closing the door silently behind her.

The knight said, "My lady, you need not have come all this way. I would have attended you downstairs, I assure you."

Lady von Berlepsch beckoned him to sit down. "I wanted to see your room so I can hold that image in my mind when I pray for your work." She held up her hands, which trembled slightly. "I can do so little else."

The knight held out his own sturdy hands. "Our Lord sees not only the work of the hands but of the heart."

The lady reached to put her hand over his. "I thank you for those kind words. I have come to ask your help in a household matter."

"I will do anything within my power."

"It is my wish that you conduct the Christmas services at the Wartburg."

Sir Georg seemed taken aback. "What does your husband think of this idea?"

The lady smiled. "He has often complained about the priests of Eisenach. How delighted he will be to hear from one whose views are closer to his own!"

Sir Georg said slowly, "I am not so sure of that, my lady. However, to please you, I will preach as many sermons as there are birds in the Thuringian Forest. I leave the matter of dealing with the captain in your capable hands."

The following day there came firm footsteps and a brisk rap at Sir Georg's door.

"Why, my dear host," said the knight, setting down his quill at once, "how good to see you. Sit down, Hans, sit down!"

Captain von Berlepsch made no move toward the chair beside the stove. "You know, of course, that the entire castle is discussing your work. From the kitchen to the armory, from the dining hall to the stable, it is 'Our *Herr Doktor* this' and "Doctor Luther that.' The soldiers are arguing points of doctrine, and the maids are gossiping about the Acts of the Apostles. You have turned my household upside-down. If those at the Wartburg speak so freely, what interesting conversations must be taking place in Eisenach, or indeed, in all of Thuringia! I dare not allow you outside these walls."

"Captain, I assure you I have no desire to go anywhere until my work here is done."

This reply did not appear to satisfy the captain. "My wife tells me that she has asked you to preach during the Christmas season."

"With your kind permission, Captain."

The captain sighed. "Martin, would it be possible for you to avoid antagonizing Dame Adela in your sermons? Up here you are blessedly alone, while I endure daily tirades about how you are destroying Christendom."

"I will do my best to keep the peace."

CHAPTER 27

Christmastide

Just before midnight on Christmas Eve the entire household of the Wartburg filed in solemn candlelit procession to the palace. The night was clear and cold. Above the castle towers the great dome of the heavens sparkled with stars as brilliant as frost flowers on a windowpane.

In the palace chapel, fires had been lit so that the vaulted chamber would be warm enough for Lady von Berlepsch, who was carried in a litter and sat wrapped in furs, Dame Adela on one side, the captain and Ilse on the other. The family von Berlepsch was flanked by Otto and Hermina. Behind them stood the soldiers of the Wartburg, their ranks diminished because some had left on holiday visits. Behind the soldiers stood Gunda and Dolf, grooms and stableboys, the gardener and the goose girl, and the other servants.

Sir Georg had put aside his knightly attire. When I first saw him standing at the altar in a plain black robe, only the glossy dark hair and beard reminded me of the man I had been called to serve. I was uncomfortable at the prospect of assisting him as altar boy, although he had tried to ease my fears.

He told me that when he celebrated his first Mass, he was so deeply awed by the divine presence in the sacramental elements and so terrified of displeasing God that his hands trembled and he nearly dropped the chalice. "But now, dear Seppel, I understand that while God is truly present in, with, and under the bread and wine, he is present in love and forgiveness. We should handle the cup reverently because we return God's love, not because we fear his punishment. Think of how carefully Hermina sets the table before the family von Berlepsch sits to dine. A priest's role is no different than that of a household servant."

I hoped that Sir Georg would not repeat that line to Dame Adela.

On that Christmas Eve in the castle Sir Georg spoke of the singing of the angels at Bethlehem: "Imagine those glorious voices echoing over the hillsides. To whom do they address their heavenly songs? Not to princes or potentates, not to those of noble birth, but to unlearned people, the lowliest of all the folk on earth. In that song to the shepherds, as in that manger bed, we see how completely God spurns that which is high and mighty in the eyes of the world!"

On Christmas Day he preached again: "And what became of those shepherds after the night in which the glory of God was revealed to them? They did not run away into the desert. They did not don monk's garb or shave their heads. Neither did they change their clothing or their schedule or their food or drink or anything else about their way of life. No, they remained shepherds.

"It was as shepherds, not as prophets or priests, that they made known to their neighbors the wonders which had been revealed to them. Those shepherds were the first preachers of the Gospel, you see. When they returned to their fields, they continued to praise and glorify God. We must remember also that as simple shepherds they continued to serve God by following their calling."

Immediately after preaching on St. Stephen's Day, Sir Georg returned to his rigorous writing routine, but the household of the Wartburg continued to celebrate Christmastide. Every day the castle gates swung open as soldiers returned and other travelers arrived to share the hospitality of the Lord of Parrots. The front hall of the Ritterhaus rang with greetings and the stomping of snow-covered boots.

One morning some of the visiting knights and squires performed feats of horsemanship in the courtyard. Ilse and I were among the spectators as a groom tossed wooden hoops high into the air and the riders speared the hoops with their swords.

Later that day, Sir Georg asked me to leave him alone to struggle with a difficult passage in his translation. I went out to the courtyard, thinking I might ask a stableboy to toss a few hoops for me. As I stood beside Tintenfleck holding a bridle, I saw Ilse standing beside her white mare, which was already saddled.

Ilse lifted her chin. "I may not have a sword, but I could catch a hoop as well as any of them. You must throw for me."

Immediately I hung up Tintenfleck's bridle.

Ilse led Eisblume toward the stable door and then halted. "No, Seppel, you should saddle Tintenfleck. We'll throw to one another."

A short time later as our horses slowly circled the yard, Ilse and I dropped our reins to keep our hands free. Each of us held a wooden hoop and watched the other's arm carefully.

"Ready?" called Ilse. "One, two, three—away!"

The hoops arced past one another in flight. I caught the one flying toward me and saw Ilse clutching the other in triumph. We both laughed aloud, and she cried, "Again!"

First we played at a walk and then at a trot. Whenever one of us missed the catch, the hoop either stuck in the sodden snow churned up by our horses' hooves or bounced and rolled on firmer ground. Ilse and I were evenly matched, for she had superior skills in horsemanship, but I had a steadier arm.

Then Ilse proposed that we gallop in figure eights and trade hoops when our horses crossed paths. My entire being was focused on the enterprise of holding my mount to the course, watching the approach, waiting, throwing, catching, then waving the hoop gleefully as Tintenfleck raced along the far edge of the figure.

Ilse missed one of my throws, and as the hoop rolled toward the castle gate she signaled Eisblume to give chase while she reached down to grab the runaway hoop. Leaning so far from the mare's back that her red-gold braid nearly touched the ground, Ilse did not see the travelers who had just come up from the underpass. When one of the men leaped forward to snatch the rolling hoop, Eisblume swerved sharply, and Ilse tumbled to the ground. For a moment after that sickening thud I stared in horror at the still figure on the trampled snow.

I breathed again when Ilse raised her head and then struggled to her feet, pulling her soiled cloak tightly about her. Her face was smeared with mud or dung, and she scowled at the travelers and said, "What are you staring at?"

One of the men was Jacoby the minstrel, and the other was the young nobleman who had sung at the royal feast. He flourished the hoop and swept an elegant bow. "I believe you dropped this, my lady."

Ilse did not smile back. She whistled for Eisblume, and when the mare trotted over to her, Ilse gathered her skirts and placed the toe of one boot inside the curve of the hoop as if it were a stirrup. The young lord grinned and raised the hoop to boost Ilse up into the saddle.

"Thank you, Peter Custodomus," she said, once again as regal as a queen.

The travelers were very merry in the dining hall of the Ritterhaus that night. I served the table at which the captain and Lady von Berlepsch presided. Peter Custodomus spent most of the evening in conversation with Ilse, but twice I caught him watching me with a curious expression. After the meal Lady von Berlepsch said, "Let us have music now, Jacoby." She turned to the young nobleman. "Peter, I am told that you are a fine singer."

Peter Custodomus said, "Where's the knight who sang at the royal feast? We must have his voice among us."

"Bring the little piper, too," said Jacoby. "Call forth Dolf of the Wartburg!"

At the captain's bidding I fetched Sir Georg, who was pleased to put down his quill at the prospect of an evening of song.

When the knight entered the dining hall, Peter Custodomus stood up and bowed. "I believe that you are more than a musician. I am honored, *Herr Doktor*. I greatly admire your work."

"Enough," said Captain von Berlepsch. "He was invited to make music, not to discuss his scribbling."

The kitchen boy appeared in the doorway, clutching his pipe and looking both timid and eager.

"Come in, Dolf! Come in!" said Sir Georg. "How good to have you here." He glanced around the room. "Seppel, fetch a lute, if you please."

When I returned with the lute, Sir Georg was standing before a row of benches. "Dolf, we need you to carry the high part with Ilse. You must sit here beside her." He nodded to Lady von Berlepsch. "My lady, you and Seppel will take the alto. Seppel, we need one more seat over there."

He took the lute from me and turned to Dame Adela, who said frostily, "I do not sing with servants."

Sir Georg smiled. "Then you have the privilege of listening to hear how well our voices blend." He beckoned to the men. "Peter

Custodomus and I will carry the tenor, and the captain and Jacoby will sing the bass. Now, my song birds, let us take it first in turns."

The knight was in a kind of rapture that night. "Are you listening to yourselves?" he said after we had run through several songs in four parts. "Do you hear how each voice is enriched by the others? Is not music one of God's finest creations?" He cradled the lute as if it were a child. "Think of the power of the Scriptures wedded to music. When we breathe together the Word of God—and you must remember that the Latin *spiritus* is "breath"—then we are truly one body, one Spirit in Christ. When commoners and kings sing hymns together, when the voices of the captain and the kitchen boy join in harmony, the very angels rejoice." He sighed with pleasure. "Perhaps I should have been a music master after all."

"You might have saved us all a great deal of trouble," the captain said.

CHAPTER 28

Farewell to the Castle

A week after Epiphany, Sir Georg sat musing over a letter from Doctor Amsdorf. "The German people must have both the New and the Old Testaments, which are the protecting wings of our Lord when he spreads his righteousness over us. But I cannot begin such an enormous task without the help of my friends. I have written to Philip, asking him to prepare a lodging for me. God willing, I will be there soon."

Another letter disturbed him greatly. "Wilder and wilder are the tales from Wittenberg. Three so-called prophets have come to town. They reject Scripture and claim to depend on individual revelation instead. Melanchthon is completely at a loss. He asks me how one can know which men are truly men of God. In such a case Duke Frederick hesitates to take action. Oh, that the elector had my faith and I his power!"

During the following weeks the knight devoted himself single-mindedly to his task. As his quill sped through the brief letters of the minor apostles toward the Revelation of St. John, my thoughts weighed heavily upon me.

When Sir Georg had first begun this project, the prospect of completing it seemed inconceivably far in the future. But now that the stacks of pages were soon to be bundled into a saddlebag, what would become of me?

Since the December journey I had known that when Sir Georg returned to Wittenberg, my make-believe knight would no longer require a make-believe page. I had no place in a world in which men argued in Latin and joked in Greek. The famous professor would have no reason to desire my presence, a reminder of his time in exile.

How soon would I be forced to strip off the attire of a page and don the clothes of a village boy? I did not know whether such clothing would fit me now. I had no chosen trade, no skills beyond a few years of schooling. Everyone else in the castle had a place here. In my head

I heard Gunda's words: "I was born at the Wartburg. I will die at the Wartburg. Let no fool keep me from my calling."

A week after the feast of St. Valentine, Sir Georg said to me, "Take this letter to the captain. I have informed Duke Frederick that I shall soon be back in Wittenberg. I must go where I am needed."

When I entered the gateroom, Captain von Berlepsch was standing at the window. He barely turned his head to acknowledge my presence. "How goes it with the scribbler?"

"Very well, sir. He has begun the sixteenth chapter of the book of Revelation."

"And how many chapters has the book of Revelation?"

"Twenty-two." I took a deep breath. "Captain, when he finishes his work and leaves the castle, what are my orders?"

The captain shrugged. "You will have no more orders. You will be free to go, as he is."

After a long pause, I said, "Should I—do you wish me to travel with him to Wittenberg?"

"You may do as you please."

I had not expected this response. "I had hoped that you would tell me what to do, sir."

Still Captain von Berlepsch did not turn to face me. "Young Burkhardt, I have no more power over you than I have over him. When you leave my household, I cannot choose your path."

Slowly I unbuckled my sword belt. The captain continued to stare out the window as I laid the sheathed weapon upon the map of Thuringia. Touching the hilt with my fingertips one last time, I said, "Thank you, sir, for entrusting me with this sword." I had never felt less like thanking him.

At last he turned to look at me. "The little black horse and his saddle and bridle—all of those belong to you."

"Thank you, sir!"

I hurried down to the stable. As I took up a brush and began to groom Tintenfleck, I remembered the words of Sir Gottfried on my

first night away from Spalt: "Faith and a good horse will carry you far."
At least I had a good horse.

For a long time after the brush was still, I stood watching the
sparrows flutter to the stable floor. Feathers fluffed against the cold,
they hopped on dainty feet to pick at fallen grain.

Sir Georg had once said that birds are our teachers and preachers,
a living example of how we are to trust in God to supply all our needs.
I stomped my feet, scattering the sparrows into the rafters.

In the front hall of the Ritterhaus, Hermina approached me, her
mouth puckered with worry. "Is it true, Seppel? Is Doctor Luther
nearly finished? Does he intend to leave soon?"

I nodded grumpily and trudged back to Sir Georg's chamber, where
I found him frowning over a half-empty page.

"I tell you, Seppel, my spirit cannot accommodate itself to this
book. This Revelation contains too little of the Gospel and too much of
the writer."

There came a knock at the door, so soft that at first I did not hear
it. Then the door opened slowly to reveal Otto. "I beg your pardon,
sir," he said, ducking his head respectfully. "I'm very sorry to disturb
your work."

Sir Georg put down his quill. "Come in, Otto, do come in. What
brings you here, my friend? A scriptural question? A theological
dispute?"

"No, sir." Otto was blushing. "*Herr Doktor*, I—that is, Hermina
and I—we think so highly of you, sir, and we do not wish to wait until
after Easter. Thus, you see, it must be done before Lent, especially now
that you are about to leave—"

I could not imagine what he was talking about.

Sir Georg smiled. "What is it you wish, Otto?"

Otto took a deep breath. "Doctor Luther, will you marry us?"

Two days later Sir Georg set down his quill and said quietly, "It is
finished." He bowed his head, and for a long stretch of time he sat in
prayer. I bowed my head and closed my eyes and tried to pray, but my
thoughts rattled in my head like a box of hazelnuts. Now Sir Georg

would go where he was needed, and I would no longer be needed anywhere.

After ending his prayer, Sir Georg sent me to fetch materials in which to wrap the completed manuscript. I left him humming cheerfully as he tidied the piles of pages. Morosely I trudged down the stairs toward the gateroom. At the foot of the stairs I found the captain and an official from Eisenach.

The official said, "His Electoral Grace has been informed that your bird intends to fly the nest." He handed a letter to the captain. "Your guest may read for himself the wishes of his Electoral Grace."

The captain directed me to take the letter to Sir Georg, who glanced at the letter and then tossed it onto the table.

"Come, Seppel, where is the oilskin I asked you to bring me for wrapping?"

He chuckled. "Look at this chapter." He pointed to smudged fingerprints and dog-ears on the fair copy I had so painstakingly transcribed. "May the German people be as eager as the household of the Wartburg to lay hands on the Word of God."

Sir Georg had nearly finished packing when Captain von Berlepsch appeared at the chamber door. Without any sort of greeting, he said, "Martin, have you read Duke Frederick's letter?"

"Indeed I have," said Sir Georg, not looking up from his task. "I shall leave tomorrow, Captain, so we must celebrate a wedding tonight."

"The elector wishes you to remain in hiding."

"Duke Frederick is a very prudent man, but sometimes he forgets that I am protected by a power greater than his."

The captain stepped into the room. "Stay a while longer, Martin. I will have your work sent to Wittenberg."

"No." Sir Georg's voice was sharp. "I will take it myself."

"And if you are captured on the way?"

For a moment the knight looked uncertain.

The captain pressed his advantage. "I will send your work with a courier while you stay here to begin translating the Old Testament."

Sir Georg scowled. "I myself will deliver these pages to a printer."

"More likely, your enemies will deliver them to a bonfire."

The knight laid his hands protectively upon the wrapped manuscript.

"Sir Georg," I began, hardly knowing what I was going to say. "Please, sir, let me carry it."

The two men stared at me.

I took a deep breath. "No one would suspect me of having anything of value. If Sir Georg were captured, I could still get the manuscript to Wittenberg."

The knight relaxed his hold upon the stack of pages. "Dear Seppel, again you come to my rescue. You and I must make this journey together."

Captain von Berlepsch did not respond at once. Then he sighed. "Pack your saddlebag, young Burkhardt. This is your last night at the Wartburg."

That evening in the dining hall Hermina and Otto stood solemnly before Sir Georg with the family von Berlepsch looking on. Even Dame Adela smiled when the knight pronounced the benediction and Hermina turned her face to her husband's for their first wedded kiss.

Lady von Berlepsch insisted that the bride and groom have the seats of honor at the banqueting-table. Gunda herself carried in the wedding supper while Dolf assisted in serving. Sir Georg offered a prayer, and then we drank to the health of the wedded couple, to safe travel, and to God's blessings on all of those gathered here.

After we had dined, Lady von Berlepsch said, "We must have a wedding dance." Sir Georg picked up the lute, and Dolf fetched his pipe. Then Otto and Hermina took hands, looking solemn again, but when the musicians struck up a lively tune, they smiled and performed a merry dance ending in an embrace applauded by us all.

"Now, Hans," said Lady von Berlepsch, "you must dance with Ilse." The captain escorted Ilse out to the floor. While our musicians played a stately sarabande, the captain and his daughter moved with suppleness and grace. As the music ended, they both bowed before Lady von Berlepsch.

"And now a circle dance for all," said the lady. Her dark-hollowed eyes seemed enormous, as if she hungered to take in everything in the room. "Gunda and Josef, take hands and join them."

In dismay I stared at the cook, who stared stonily back at me. Slowly I extended my hand and performed my most courtly bow. To my surprise, *Frau* Gunda lifted up the corners of her apron and curtsied to me. Then Sir Georg tapped out the count, Dolf piped the opening notes, and I forgot my reluctance to join the dance. My partner and I were not well-matched in size, but she moved lightly and kept perfect time.

During our brief alliance Gunda neither smiled nor frowned. At the end of the tune we changed partners. Otto bowed to Ilse, Hermina took hands with me, and to the delight of the rest of the household, the captain became partner to the cook. Hermina beamed at everyone in the room.

When the tune came around once more, the captain was paired with Hermina, Otto with Gunda, and I with Ilse. The two of us stood so close that I could smell cinnamon and cloves on her breath. Ilse danced with superb control, every move deliberate and sure. She never lost herself in the music as Hermina did, but Ilse did smile at me that night. Even now I remember the firm clasp of her slender fingers, toughened by the leather of the reins.

After the dancing, Lady von Berlepsch seemed exhausted, and Dame Adela urged her to retire. The lady beckoned Sir Georg and me to her side. When the knight knelt beside her chair, she whispered a few words to him and put her hand over his as he murmured a reply. Sir Georg lifted her hand to his lips, then made the sign of the cross upon her forehead. When the knight rose and stepped away from her, I knelt as he had done.

Lady von Berlepsch pushed back my hair, and I felt the touch of her lips upon my forehead. "I may not see you again in this world, dear child, but I know we shall meet in the next."

Dame Adela's parting words were more blunt. "I fear for your soul, boy. Be careful of the company you keep."

Hermina wept and hugged me when she said farewell. Too choked up to speak, Otto slapped me on the back and pumped Sir Georg's arm repeatedly before he fled the room with his tearful bride.

Before dawn the next morning, Dolf handed me a package of provisions, which I slid into my saddlebag with the wrapped manuscript. The kitchen boy looked wistfully at the knight standing beside his horse. "I'll miss you and your music, sir."

"Dolf of the Wartburg, you will never be without the blessings of music." Sir Georg looked at the kitchen doorway, where Gunda stood with her arms crossed. "Many thanks, good *Frau*! May the Lord continue to bless the work of your hands."

Gunda actually smiled. "And yours, *Herr Doktor*," she said.

Sir Georg and I rode out of the castle accompanied by Captain von Berlepsch and Ilse. During the steep trek down the mountainside, the silence was broken only by the thudding of hooves and the morning calls of birds. When we entered the forest, the last stars glittered above us like a net of jewels caught in the bare branches. In the distance I could see the rise of the great cleft rock. I wondered whether I would ever again visit the Dragon's Gorge.

At the ridge where the road to Jena sloped down into the wooded valley, the captain pulled up his horse along Sir Georg's chestnut. "This is as far as we go," he said, holding out his hand to the knight. "Martin, it has been an honor indeed."

"My dear Hans, admirable host and friend, how can I thank you for all you have done?"

"Your continued safety would be thanks enough."

The captain turned to me and reached out his right hand to clasp mine. "You have served him well, Josef Burkhardt, and thus you have served me. I am in your debt."

"Oh no, sir!" There was much I wanted to say, but I had to keep my jaw set firm.

Sir Georg seemed at a loss as to how to express his affection for Ilse. He managed to maneuver his horse close to hers, and for a moment I feared he might lose his seat in an attempt to kiss her hand.

However, Ilse expertly nudged the white mare alongside the chestnut and leaned over to kiss the knight's cheek. "Dear *Herr Doktor*, may God bless you as you have blessed us."

Sir Georg seemed quite overcome.

Then Ilse brought Eisblume alongside Tintenfleck. Letting go of the reins, she pulled back the edge of her riding cloak to reveal a sword belt. Deftly she unbuckled the belt and held the sheathed weapon aloft. "Here, Seppel. Catch it if you can!"

She tossed the sword, belt and all, and instinctively I caught it by the sheathed blade. With wonder I grasped the familiar hilt of the sword.

I glanced at Captain von Berlepsch, but Ilse lifted her chin. "The sword is mine to give, and I have made my choice."

Then the white mare reared, almost dancing on her hind legs.

Ilse called, "Father, I'll meet you at the Dragon's Gorge!" A moment later she and Eisblume were out of sight among the trees.

Captain von Berlepsch gave Sir Georg a final salute.

The last we heard of the captain and his daughter was the sound of galloping hooves on the forest trail.

CHAPTER 29

Another Journey

I soon forgot the bittersweet parting in the excitement of a new adventure. I rode with confidence, my sword at my side and the New Testament in my saddlebag. On this first day of March, signs of the changing season were everywhere. New grass peeped through the last patches of snow. Tiny buds were swelling on the branches overhead, and the air was brisk and fresh as a change in the wind. Riding through the vast forest on a good horse in the company of a dear friend, how could anyone feel less than pure exhilaration?

For several hours Sir Georg and I rode side by side on the road to Erfurt. Towards evening the knight said, "Since Epiphany, this day's ride is the longest stretch of hours I have spent without a pen in my hand." He flexed his fingers. "Still, my mind has not been idle on the road. Do you know, Seppel, that time away from work is essential to accomplishing the work itself? In the rhythm of the seasons or the shift from daylight to darkness, God refreshes the body and the mind."

He sighed. "Remember that quiet pool at the Dragon's Gorge? I often remember that moment and the psalmist's words: 'Be still, and know that I am God.' My time in exile has taught me how important it is to listen for the fulfillment of the Word as well as to shout for others to hear."

When we came to open country, our horses trudged along muddy wagon ruts, hooves sinking to the frozen soil below. After a day of such toil the horses were so weary that we turned into an innyard outside Jena well before dark. The inn was small and the yard well-kept, and the brightly-painted sign bore a picture of a black bear. As I tended to the horses, Tintenfleck guzzled his grain, looking comical with barley kernels clinging to his whiskers. Hearing sparrows in the rafters, I brushed the grains from Tintenfleck's muzzle onto the stable floor. Then I slung the saddlebag over my shoulder and entered the inn.

Sir Georg sat on a bench near the fireplace. After wiping the mud from my boots, I took a seat beside him. I slid the saddlebag under the bench and stretched my legs toward the fire. My body ached, and I was content to stare into the flames. The innkeeper brought a tankard without my asking. He looked me over keenly, and I wondered what he saw that could be of any special interest.

Other guests were drinking deeply and joking about the lean and sober days to come. Back in Spalt my mother and sisters would be enjoying the feasting that preceded the Lenten season. Each cottage near the tannery would contribute the last of the winter meat to a hearty stew, and the neighbors would gorge themselves until Ash Wednesday.

A few patrons departed, and Sir Georg and I moved to the table they had left. To my dismay the knight took out a book and set it upon the table. I glanced around the room, but the other guests showed no interest in the lone knight. Through half-closed eyes I studied my companion. The scarlet slouch cap was bright against his dark hair, and he had one hand upon the book and the other upon the hilt of his sword. I wondered how many more times I would see him carry a sword.

The outer door opened, and a cold draft swept into the room. Two plainly dressed travelers entered. They stomped the mud from their boots and spoke quietly to one another. At last they both squatted on a low bench just inside the door.

When Sir Georg looked up from his reading, he beckoned to the newcomers. "Come in, come in, friends. Sit here with me, if you please."

"Sir," I whispered, "please put away your book."

The knight ignored me as the travelers shuffled meekly over to our table.

"Innkeeper," called the knight, "bring wine for my guests."

Sir Georg was delighted to learn that the travelers were Swiss students on their way to Wittenberg. "I have many friends at the university," he told them.

I glared at the knight, but he did not look in my direction.

One of the students said eagerly, "Oh, sir, can you tell us whether Martin Luther is now at Wittenberg—or where he might be?"

Sir Georg smiled. "He is not now in Wittenberg, but I sincerely hope he will get there soon."

I tried to catch his eye and signal him to stop speaking so freely. The innkeeper was lurking near our table, though the tankards and wine-cups were full.

Sir Georg's words began pouring out as if a dam had burst. He spoke of the work of Philip Melanchthon and other professors. He used Latin phrases for humor or to clarify a point, nodding sagely when the students appreciated his wit.

One of the young men flipped open the little book on the table, then looked at the knight in awe. "You read Hebrew, sir?"

"Of course," said the knight. "I find great comfort in the Psalms, and most translations fail to capture the spirit of the poetry." He lowered his voice and said, "Now tell me, friends, what do the Swiss think of Luther?"

Still Sir Georg refused to look at me.

I fixed my steely gaze on the nearby innkeeper. "Go about your business," I said. "I'll call you when we're ready to dine."

As Sir Georg and the Swiss students and I were finishing our meal, two merchants entered the inn. When they had removed their cloaks and spurs, the innkeeper showed them to our table. One of the merchants set a package on the table and removed the wrapping to reveal the unbound pages of a book. He said proudly, "This is Doctor Luther's exposition of several Gospels and Epistles, just off the press."

He spoke so boldly that I thought Luther's enemies must have sent him here to entrap us. The Swiss students exclaimed in delight and asked the merchant's permission to examine the book. I willed Sir Georg to look at me that I might warn him silently to take no interest in the book.

But the knight said to his companions, "How good it is to have these new explanations of the Scriptures available to the German people. The present generation must be weaned from the sour milk of error, for that is all they know from birth. We must ensure that our own children are raised on the rich and wholesome goodness of the pure Word of God."

The second merchant nodded. "I don't understand much of this new theology. But the way things look to me, this man Luther must be an angel from heaven or a devil from hell. I'd like to meet him."

"Let us drink to Martin Luther," said the first merchant. "Angel or devil or man of God, may he live to reap the fruits of his labor."

Immediately the students raised their wine-cups.

I knew that Sir Georg did not dare to catch my eye as he gave a hearty "Amen!"

On Ash Wednesday we passed through villages in which the foreheads of everyone we saw were marked with the dark smudge of ashes. When we entered the town of Borna, Sir Georg said, "According to the captain, Duke Frederick has a representative here. I hope he will be kind enough to send a letter for me."

At the door of the electoral office the servant said with chilling formality, "Whom shall I say is calling?"

"A friend of the Lord of Parrots," said Sir Georg serenely.

A few moments later a finely-dressed official appeared at the door. "*Gott im Himmel!*" he said, immediately lowering his voice. "What are you doing here?"

After his initial shock the electoral representative treated us quite well. For the first time since we had left the Wartburg, I relaxed my hold upon the saddlebag. When Sir Georg asked for paper and ink, the official invited the knight to use his own desk. I listened to the scratching of the quill, waiting for the knight to push back his chair and read aloud what he had written. I wondered how many more times I was to hear that voice address me with such intimacy.

There came the scraping of the chair. "Now, my dear Seppel, you must listen to this."

> I have served your Electoral Grace well enough by staying in hiding for a year. The devil knows very well that I did not hide from cowardice, for he saw my heart when I entered the city of Worms. Had I known then that as many devils were lying in wait for me as there are tiles on the roofs, I should nevertheless have leaped into their midst with joy.

The knight read as fiercely as if Satan himself were sitting in the chair opposite. "I would go through Leipzig even if it rained Duke Georges for nine days, and every duke were nine times as furious as this one."

I stared at him. "Go through Leipzig, sir? But that is Duke George's territory. He has sworn himself your enemy."

The knight seemed unperturbed. "We will save a day's journey by cutting through Leipzig."

"But, sir, even Duke Frederick has no power there."

Sir Georg folded the letter carefully. "I have informed his Grace that he is to consider himself freed from any responsibility for my safety."

In the company of an outlaw who prided himself on opposing the will of his own protector, there was nothing I could do except pray for us both.

CHAPTER 30

Among the Enemy

Late in the day we arrived at Leipzig. When we entered the south gate of the city, I was very aware of the height and breadth of the walls surrounding us. However, we rode through the winding streets without incident. I breathed a prayer of thanks when we passed out of the north gate into the countryside. I urged Tintenfleck into a trot so that we might put a few more miles between ourselves and the palace of a powerful enemy.

When at last we turned into an innyard, I said to Sir Georg, "I wish you would not read at the table tonight."

He did not respond with a light remark, as I had expected. When he remained with me in the stable as I tended to the horses, I saw that he acknowledged the extent of our danger.

I held the saddlebag tight as we entered the inn. In deference to the penitential season the guests were subdued. I would have preferred them to be making merry instead of falling silent to stare at us as we took our places at a table.

Sir Georg kept his head low. By all appearances he was a weary traveler who did not care to be disturbed. The innkeeper brought us a meal of plain fare. The knight and I ate quickly and spoke little, occasionally glancing toward the door when newcomers entered. The other travelers were mostly merchants or students. In fact, Sir Georg and I were the only members of the nobility in the establishment until another knight entered, followed closely by his squire.

The squire peered sharply around the room, and almost instantly his eyes met mine. Impossible as it seemed, I recognized that face. Too late I turned away, for the squire was Erich, with whom I had once crossed swords. The grizzled knight made his way to our table. Whether or not he recognized me, Sir Gottfried obviously chose to sit with another man of rank.

He bowed slightly to Sir Georg. "May I join you?"

Sir Georg rose to acknowledge the bow. "It would be my pleasure."

The other knight's entry had created a stir of interest in the room. I hoped I looked unconcerned as the squire sat across the table from me. Remembering our last encounter, I half-expected Erich to spit some accusation, but he barely glanced at me.

But Sir Gottfried looked directly at me before he spoke again to my companion. "I wish you safe travel. You will find that loyal subjects of Duke George need have no fear of highwaymen. Royal officers are stationed all along the main roads. No outlaw could hope to remain at large for long."

"That gives me great comfort," said Sir Georg. "I look forward to a pleasant journey." Abruptly he asked a question about Sir Gottfried's sword. The grizzled knight showed him the intricately wrought hilt and the fine blade. He told the story of its making and provided a general discourse on the art of metalcraft. I listened politely, my gaze fixed on Sir Gottfried so that I would not accidentally exchange glances with Erich.

At last Sir Georg called for the innkeeper and paid our bill. After wishing our companions a restful night, we retired to the sleeping quarters. Other men were already asleep in the room, and I had no opportunity to talk privately to Sir Georg.

As I turned restlessly on my pallet on the floor, my head pillowed on the saddlebag, I tried to figure out how the other knight and his squire had tracked us here. It was no accident that they had come to this inn on this night—of that I was certain.

At last I fell into a fitful sleep, and I dreamed that I was riding through a dark forest, clutching the manuscript in my arms. Rain fell and the wind blew, and great wet blotches appeared on the pages, and the ink smeared and ran. Whole chapters were torn away by the wind while I snatched at empty air. The lost papers whirled madly around me as if demons had set them to dancing, and even the wind began to speak in a mocking whisper: "Seppel, Seppel, you fool, you fool!"

I sat up to find myself in the dark chamber. Sir Georg was still snoring, but close beside me I heard a soft hiss like the demonic breath of the wind. Then came a slight rustling, and my arm shot out and grabbed something soft—a garment. I was about to cry out when my captive hissed, "Keep quiet, you fool! Sir Gottfried has sent me. The Leipzig spies know about your so-called knight. Wake him and come to the stable. We must flee at once."

Erich wrenched his sleeve from my grip and slipped soundlessly out of the room. Hardly knowing whether I was awake or dreaming, I reached for the saddlebag, which was reassuringly solid beneath my hand.

I woke Sir Georg and whispered to him what had happened.

He whispered back, "Do you trust this Gottfried?"

"Yes, sir, but I'm not sure I trust the squire."

"What do you think we should do?"

"I don't know, sir. What if this is a trap?"

Sir Georg was silent for a moment, and then he murmured, "I believe that God has sent these men to us. If we are trapped, God can free us from the snare, if it is his will."

We rummaged in the darkness for our belongings. Then I slung the saddlebag over my shoulder, and we groped our way through the darkened inn to the moonlit yard, where two horsemen stood. A groom yawned from the doorway of the stable, where he held the reins of our saddled horses. Sir Gottfried tossed a coin to the groom, who was not too sleepy to catch it.

Without speaking, we mounted our horses and followed the grizzled knight and his squire out of the yard into the night. The moon was low in the west, the faint light glancing from the fittings of Tintenfleck's bridle. Soon we turned off the main road onto a wagon lane that narrowed to a cow path through a meadow. Mile after mile we covered at the same steady gait, while the calling of the night birds gave way to the song of the lark. We rode past cottages where herdsmen and milkmaids paused in their morning chores to stare at the passing noblemen.

Hour after hour we rode, hardly speaking, keeping always in single file, Sir Gottfried before us and Erich behind.

The sun was high overhead when Sir Gottfried reined in his horse long enough to gesture toward the horizon. "Electoral Saxony lies just beyond the river. We will escort you across the bridge and then ride ahead to see that no other danger lies between you and Wittenberg."

He took the lead again with Sir Georg behind him, and the squire fell back to follow me. Once more Sir Georg and I were securely flanked as we traversed the narrow road toward the river. When our horses' hooves clattered over the wooden bridge, I breathed a prayer of thanks that in spite of Sir Georg's foolhardiness, we had come safely through enemy territory.

We stopped to rest our horses and share our provisions with our companions. As Sir Georg offered the last of the Wartburg bread, he said, "So, my guardian angels, who sent you, apart from the God who protects us all?"

Sir Gottfried said, "The elector's man at Borna gave word that you were on the road to Leipzig."

I turned to Erich. "But how did you find us?"

"We searched every stable along the main road." The squire was as smug as ever. "I'd know that little black horse anywhere."

As Sir Gottfried mounted his horse, he said, "Go with God, my fellow swordsmen."

"God keep you both!" called Sir Georg, and then we watched the evening shadows swallow the other knight and his squire.

At twilight we approached a little red-roofed town surrounded by an ancient wall. I was tired from the long day of travel, and Tintenfleck's neck was lathered with sweat, but I rode easily in the saddle. Ahead of me poor Sir Georg looked much more uncomfortable. I amused myself by remembering the journey from Spalt when I had bounced along like a plow boy. Had I arrived at the Wartburg only ten months ago? The seasons before I entered that mountaintop fortress seemed a lifetime away.

Suddenly a sharp voice rang out. A band of horsemen rode from behind the town wall. I had a confused notion that they had somehow sprung from the roof tiles.

"Halt, if you value your lives!" growled the masked rider in the lead.

The other riders positioned themselves to block our path. There were perhaps eight or ten of them, all masked, all with swords drawn. Had the squire betrayed us? Whatever the reason, we had been captured as easily as rabbits dangling in a snare.

Sir Georg was ahead of me, facing the row of horsemen. If only he would turn his head, I might be able to signal him, but to do what? To turn our horses and flee? To draw our swords and attempt to fight our way out?

A second rider spoke. "That's the man all right."

"How can you be sure?" asked the leader.

"I've seen his portrait."

The other riders maneuvered their horses into a tight circle around us. I felt sickening despair. Captain von Berlepsch had been right after all. How stupid of that painter in Wittenberg to portray the outlaw as a knight.

The second rider said, "He's uglier than the picture. I don't understand why Cranach would waste a canvas."

The leader chuckled. "Perhaps he pitied the poor fellow."

They grinned under their masks, and I hated them for their arrogance. The other riders called bantering remarks to their comrades, and Sir Georg turned in the saddle to look at me. At the anguish in his face I put my hand to the hilt of my sword.

Instantly his face changed. "No, Seppel! *Impero fugere!*"

The order to flee only paralyzed me. How could I abandon this innocent man to his enemies? I wrenched my sword free from the sheath.

"Not that one!" barked the knight. "*Gladius spiritum!* The sword of the Spirit!"

Abruptly he unsheathed his own sword and began waving it wildly, shouting Latin phrases I could not understand as his startled horse reared, almost unseating him. As the other riders moved in on him, brandishing their weapons, I signaled Tintenfleck to back up, and in the confusion we broke free from the circle. As Tintenfleck turned, I dug my heels into his sides, laying the flat of my sword against his flanks as we galloped down off the roadway and plunged into the forest.

Bending low over Tintenfleck's neck, I closed my eyes and trusted my horse to get me through the dark wood. Over the sound of galloping hooves and the swish and scratching of tree branches, I could not hear whether we were pursued. A sob caught in my throat as I prayed aloud: "Spare him, dear God, please spare him! O Lord, I will bear anything, anything, if only you let him do his holy work!"

CHAPTER 31

In the Market Square

In a clearing I reined Tintenfleck to a halt. Apart from my horse's labored breathing, I heard only the distant lowing of cattle. I heard no human voices, no sounds of pursuit. I was utterly alone.

If only Sir Georg had listened to Captain von Berlepsch. . . . If only I had not volunteered to carry the manuscript. . . . If only Sir Georg had not insisted on traveling through Leipzig. . . .

Such futile and bitter thoughts assailed me in the darkness. What would become of the outlaw at the hands of his enemies? If I rode in search of him, how could I possibly rescue him from an armed band? Remembering Sir Georg's desperate shouts, I knew he would not want me to risk myself or the precious contents of my saddlebag.

I must ride to Wittenberg and deliver the manuscript to Master Melanchthon or Doctor Amsdorf. Surely the two of them would enlist the help of the outlaw's powerful friends to organize a search party. I patted Tintenfleck's lathered neck and looked up at the night sky to get my bearings. If I could get back to the main road, I might recognize some of the landmarks from our December journey to Wittenberg.

I nudged Tintenfleck toward the distant sound of cattle, and we struck a cowpath that led to a farmstead near the outskirts of a village, where a watchman told me that Wittenberg was only a few miles away. Thanking God for moonlight, I pressed Tintenfleck into a gallop down the long road.

When at last the dark rim of the town wall appeared, I saw light flickering within the open gates. Had someone already roused the residents of Wittenberg? As Tintenfleck and I entered the gates, I resisted the impulse to shout out the true name of the outlaw and ask these strangers for help. Even now I had to keep my friend's secret until I found someone I could trust.

We trotted past the Castle Church to the market square, where a group of horsemen was surrounded by a crowd of men and boys with torches. I recognized the building behind them as Cranach House. Surely the wealthy painter could summon the necessary forces.

Reining in Tintenfleck, I said to one of the boys, "Where is Lucas Cranach? I must speak to him at once."

The boy gestured toward the crowd. "He's over there with *Herr* Doerring, sir."

Seeing the painter standing beside the goldsmith, I urged Tintenfleck through the crowd. Without dismounting, I called, "*Herr* Cranach! Please, sir, I need your help. Sir Georg has been captured!"

The painter squinted up at me. "Who is Sir Georg? And who might you be?"

I gaped at him. "Please, *Herr* Cranach! I'm Seppel from—from the Kingdom of the Birds. I met you when I came here with—" I dropped my voice and hissed—"Martin Luther."

"Martin Luther?" said Cranach loudly. He nudged the goldsmith and grinned. "Well, why didn't you say so?"

He seemed so cheerful that I thought he must have lost his mind.

In desperation I turned to the goldsmith. "*Herr* Doerring, your friend Luther has been captured by highwaymen. They can't be too far away. We have to find him, sir."

To my astonishment the goldsmith slapped Cranach on the back and said, "No, they certainly can't be too far away."

Were they both complete fools? "We have to find him," I repeated.

"You needn't look far," said Cranach. "He's right over there."

I stared at the painter and then turned to look more closely at the other men in the market square. Sitting on horseback in the middle of the crowd was Sir Georg, smiling and nodding to those who spoke to him. In the flickering torchlight, he appeared more knightly than ever before.

I dropped the reins, cupped my hands to my mouth, and shouted as loudly as I could: "Sir Georg! Sir Georg!"

Instantly his expression changed, and when he saw me, he said, "*Gott sei dank*! Dear Seppel, you are safe and well!"

Heedless of everything else around me, I rode Tintenfleck through the crowd till I could reach out and grasp the knight's outstretched hand.

"How did you escape, sir?"

Sir Georg chuckled. "The masked men were no highwaymen. Those rascals Cranach and Doerring caught me out this time. What a fine trick they played on us, Seppel. A fine trick indeed."

A trick. For a moment I felt dizzy, and then anger surged through my entire body. I was angrier at Sir Georg than at his friends. How could he laugh at what they had done? Didn't he understand how carelessly they had played with our lives on that lonely road? I remembered my desperate prayer during that terrifying flight through the woods. A fine trick indeed.

Sir Georg dismounted, and I lost sight of him in the pressing throng of well-wishers with their cries of "*Willkommen, Herr Doktor!*" and "Our champion has returned!"

I dismounted so abruptly that Tintenfleck sidestepped in alarm. When a stableboy offered to take the reins, I said sharply, "Step aside. I'll see to my own horse."

By the time I finished rubbing down Tintenfleck, my anger had subsided, and in its place I felt only a dull ache. Slinging the saddlebag over my shoulder, I walked to the door of Cranach House and said to the servant, "Take me to the knight called Georg."

The servant retreated and whispered with another, then returned to the doorway and said, "*Herr Doktor* Luther has already retired for the night. Would you care for a meal or should I show you to your chamber?"

I was suddenly so exhausted that I could not imagine sitting upright any longer. In the bedchamber I unbuckled my sword and took off my cloak and boots. From old habit I pillowed my head on the saddlebag. Sir Georg had not even thought to ask about his precious manuscript. For some time I lay awake, listening to footsteps in the corridor and the murmur of voices, and at last I fell into a dreamless sleep.

When I awoke the next morning, I reached to touch the worn leather of the saddlebag. I looked around the unfamiliar room, slowly remembering how I had come to be here. I decided to put the manuscript into Sir Georg's hands immediately. I dressed quickly, hesitating briefly before donning my sword. Who knew how much longer I would have the opportunity to wear it?

Then I slung the saddlebag over my shoulder and walked out into the long corridor. Cranach House was enormous, and I had no idea how to find the knight. I saw a monk standing in a doorway, so I stepped forward to ask him.

"Good morning," I said. "I'm looking for the man known as Sir Georg."

The monk bowed his head gravely and pointed to the floor of the chamber. "There is all that is left of him."

Shining black curls were strewn over the slate like the aftermath of a sheep-shearing. Shocked, I stared again at the monk and saw merriment in the keen dark eyes.

He rubbed his clean-shaven chin and ran a hand through his cropped hair. "Ah, Seppel, you cannot imagine how good it feels to look like myself again."

"No, sir, I cannot," I said, trying to hide my dismay.

"And see what you have brought me!" Eagerly the monk took the saddlebag from me. I followed him into the room and watched him pull out the wrapped manuscript. He raised the bundle jubilantly. "Dear Seppel, you have been my swordbearer indeed. Soon I will put this weapon into the hands of others, that they may defend themselves again the devil, the world, and the flesh."

He tossed the empty saddlebag to the floor. "I must take this to Philip at once. He and I have much work to do."

"And what should I do, sir?"

"I'm sure Cranach can find something useful for you. He keeps any number of men and boys employed in one thing or another. The workshop, the printing press, the apothecary—Lucas Cranach has a finger in every pie in Wittenberg."

Humming to himself, the monk hurried away down the corridor, leaving me standing among the last traces of the friend I had known.

I picked up the saddlebag. Clutching it tightly, I wandered blindly down the corridors of Cranach House. I blundered into doorways, for what did it matter whether I behaved badly now? Bitterly I reflected that my prayer had indeed been answered. Had I not assured God that I could bear anything if only this man could continue his holy work?

Turning a corner, I nearly ran into a well-dressed younger boy.

He brushed off my apology and said, "I remember you from your visit in December. I could hardly keep from laughing to see Doctor Luther pretending to be a knight."

Vaguely I remembered him as the painter's son, who had shown me the workshop. "I have never known him except as a knight."

Instantly the smile disappeared. "How strange this must be for you."

His sympathy gave me courage to say, "Doctor Luther is not the only pretender. I'm no son of nobility. Do you know where I could find some different clothes?"

He grinned. "As long as you don't mind a few spots of paint."

The dining hall of Cranach House was as crowded as a crossroads inn. Workmen, artisans, apprentices, and servants all sat at long tables in a room filled with voices and laughter. I had hardly taken in the scene when a woman in a white cap and apron called to me, "Welcome, my dear boy, welcome to Cranach House. Sit down here beside me. My husband tells me his silly prank frightened you terribly last night. I must apologize for him, as he will never do so himself. I hope you will forgive him."

Herr Cranach fixed me with a grave look under his bushy eyebrows. "Come now, young Burkhardt. I will ask your pardon since my Barbara insists upon it."

I mumbled something in return, feeling as awkward as during my first encounter with the family von Berlepsch. An ache of longing for the Wartburg swept over me.

The painter continued cheerfully, "You can put away your sword, young Burkhardt. At Cranach House we could find more use for a broom."

CHAPTER 32

The Kingdom of the Word

After leaving the dining hall, I visited Tintenfleck in the stable, where my change of clothing must have mystified the stableboy even more. Then I wandered around inside Cranach House, waiting for someone to tell me what to do. As I stood in the doorway of the workshop, one of the artisans said, "Here, boy. Sweep the floor."

I found a broom and hurried to obey. As I leaned to reach stray shavings under a table, the bright blue eyes of the old blockcutter met mine. "You do your work well," he said, his manner no different than when I had appeared before him as a young nobleman. I sighed as I dropped the sweepings into a basket of kindling, glad that Ilse von Berlepsh could not see me now.

When I entered the press room with my broom, the printer snapped, "We can't have you raising dust around the press!" Chastened, I stood in the doorway watching one of the workers reach deftly into the two cases of metal type. He never took his eyes from the manuscript tacked to an easel as he arranged the type in a small tray in his other hand.

Noting my interest, the printer's expression softened. "Have you never seen a press before?"

"No, sir."

"That's the compositor. After he builds up enough lines of type on the composing stick, he moves them to a galley tray, which holds one page. For a quarto like this, we lock four pages into a frame. Then we place the frame onto the imposing stone." He waved his hand in dismissal. "Now do your sweeping elsewhere."

The next morning the entire Cranach household crossed the Market Square to worship in the Town Church. It seemed that all of Wittenberg had turned out to hear Doctor Luther preach on the first Sunday of Lent. In the crowd, I became separated from the Cranachs and found myself surrounded by strangers.

An excited murmur rose from the worshipers when the black-haired monk ascended the pulpit. I might not have recognized the distant figure, but his voice was unmistakable.

"The summons of death comes to us all," he said. A silence fell over the crowd. Luther let the silence grow almost unbearable before he spoke again: "And each must fight his own battle alone. Therefore, everyone must be armed for the battle. Everyone must know for himself the chief things that concern a Christian. We should all be well-versed in the Bible and able to confront the devil with many passages."

Again he fell silent and stood looking out over the congregation. "From all accounts, many of you are quite ready to confront the devil or anyone else. I notice that you have a great deal to say of the doctrine of faith and love, and this is no wonder. Even an ass can intone the lessons. You have used your knowledge of Scripture not to build up but to destroy the work of God's kingdom. What has become of order? Wanton actions with no regard for proper order are offensive to your neighbors and thus offensive to God."

His tone changed from scornful to sorrowful. "Without love, faith is nothing, as the Apostle Paul tells us. And here, my friends, have you not grievously failed? Here in Wittenberg I see no signs of love among you. God does not want merely hearers and repeaters of words but followers and doers, and this occurs in faith through love."

"Dear friends, whoever has true faith does not insist upon his own rights but looks to see what may be helpful to his neighbor. If we do not show love to our neighbors, as our Lord Jesus has taught us, our work will not long endure. Therefore I could no longer remain away but was compelled to come and say these things to you."

After the service I had no desire to move in for a closer look at the famous preacher. How foolish I had been to think that the hero of Germany might still have time for me. I bowed my head and trudged back to the stable to see faithful Tintenfleck.

The following morning Doctor Luther preached again, and in the afternoon a servant of Cranach House told me I had a visitor. Hurrying to the portrait chamber, I was disappointed to find a stranger instead of my friend of the Wartburg. Yet the well-dressed figure studying the painting on an easel was oddly familiar, and when he turned, for a moment I thought I was in the presence of my father. Immediately I realized my mistake. "Uncle—Uncle Spalatin?"

The man smiled and came forward to embrace me. Then he stood looking at me, his hands on my shoulders. "Dear Josef, how very like your father you are." Stepping back, he gestured toward a chair. "On behalf of his Grace the Elector, I commend you for your service to Saxony."

I waited for him to sit down before I took my seat.

"And on behalf of the family Burkhardt," my uncle continued, "I have arranged for you to finish your schooling in Spalt, according to your father's wishes. If you are successful, there will be a place for you at the university of Wittenberg."

I could not think clearly. Go back to St. Nicholas School? That world seemed a lifetime away. Something else tugged at my mind, and I remembered Annchen's plaintive words, "Mama, are we selling Seppel?"

"Uncle, I can't attend school when my family is in need. I must find work instead."

"I'm pleased to hear you say that, Josef, but you need have no concerns about money. My brother Stefan and I have reached an understanding about the family business. The tannery will pay a small pension to your mother. Stefan has assured me that this allowance will continue throughout her lifetime."

For so long I had assumed that whatever I could earn would be needed at home that I hardly knew how to respond.

"I've arranged for you to travel home with some merchants bound for Nuremberg. Let us hope that your journey tomorrow is less eventful than others you have made."

I stood up politely as Uncle Spalatin left the room, but as soon as he was gone, I sank heavily into the chair. The man I had served was safe, and my family was provided for. I could return to a classroom instead of carrying a broom. My prayers had been answered, so why did the neat ordering of my life leave me so dissatisfied?

Morosely I stared at the paintings in various stages of completion. On one canvas the head and shoulders of a figure seemed to float in a void. On another, a landscape had been lightly sketched in. On the third, I saw an exquisitely painted corner of blue sky.

I left the chamber and walked slowly down the corridor. Hearing the steady thump of the printing press, I stopped at the threshold to watch one worker rock two ink balls over the locked frame on the imposing stone while another laid a sheet of dampened paper over the other surface of the press. Then the two men took turns cranking to press the paper onto the frame. When the press opened, one of the men pulled off the inked sheet, holding it carefully by the edges.

The printer beckoned me into the room. "There, boy. What do you think of this proof sheet?"

At the sight of the perfect columns of crisp black letters, I felt an ache of longing so strong that I could not even speak. Soon Doctor Luther's words, copied in my own hand, would be thus transformed. And while the Word of God was printed for the German people in this very room, I would be sitting among schoolboys as they fidgeted over Latin verbs.

With a sigh I began to read the first column. Then I squinted at the text. "Sir," I said hesitantly, "the fifth line seems to be missing a word."

The printer smiled. "Do you have dreams of trading a broom for a turn at the press?" He peered at the page, then looked at me again. "What else do you see?" His voice was sharp.

Blushing, I began to read the words slowly to myself. "I see a space missing—just there." I pointed, careful not to touch the damp sheet.

"You have a good eye." The printer looked more closely at me. "Aren't you Luther's boy? Martin said he had a scribe during his time away. You should be reading proof. What do you say to that?"

"I leave tomorrow for Franconia."

"That's too bad. Let me see now. Hans Sachs has a printshop in Nuremberg. You might look him up. Tell him Melchior Lotther sent you."

By the time I thought to say, "Thank you, sir," *Herr* Lotther had turned back to his work.

That evening at Cranach House as I knelt to say my prayers, I remembered that no coins or prayers could affect my father now. The only way I could honor him was by becoming the man he had wanted me to become. For his sake I must try to overcome this strange reluctance to return to the place I had once called home. Thanks to Uncle Spalatin, I would be able to fulfill my father's dream for me. Then why did I feel so ungrateful?

In the gray light of dawn I waited for the merchants to assemble. Tintenfleck stood ready beside me, the saddlebag stocked with provisions from *Frau* Cranach. The market square was dim and still, but I knew one man who would already be turning to his morning's task. Surely my friend of the Wartburg would have time for a quick farewell. I mounted Tintenfleck, and we trotted down the street past the goldsmith's shop and Master Melanchthon's house to the monastery called the Black Cloister.

Dismounting at the gate, I walked up an overgrown garden path to the door. My heart was beating absurdly fast. Back at the Wartburg, Sir Georg had spoken of this place so often that I knew exactly how to find his study. I entered the building, climbed a winding stair, and crossed a small room to a door, which stood open just enough to allow me to see that dear figure sitting at a desk. Timidly I knocked upon the door.

"Ah, there you are, Seppel," he said absently. "Philip has found some of my lines too poetic. He has ruined this fair copy. You must make a new one for the printer."

Mouth open, I entered the room and took the pages from Doctor Luther's outstretched hand. Sitting down at a table, I stared at the pages before me. There in my own hand was the Gospel of Matthew again. I arranged the blank sheet squarely upon the table, dipped the quill into the inkwell, and thanked God for giving me one last opportunity to serve.

We worked in a companionable silence, as in the old days, the only sound in the room the delicate scratching of our pens. I finished one page, laid it aside, and took up another. My quill moved smoothly over the paper, copying the words of our Lord in his sermon to the multitudes:

> "Ask, and it shall be given you;
> Seek, and ye shall find;
> Knock, and the door shall be opened unto you."

My pen stopped moving.

At that very moment Doctor Luther set down his quill and stared at me. "My dear Seppel, I fear I have delayed your departure. I slipped into my old habit quite without thinking. Please forgive me."

I took a deep breath. "*Herr Doktor*," I said, though the phrase felt awkward as I spoke it, "I do not wish to go. I want to help you in your work."

He blinked. "But Spalatin told me he had made suitable arrangements for you. He said that you would be able to continue your schooling."

"Why should I go back to school?" I rose to my feet, still clutching the quill.

"Seppel, why would you forgo such an opportunity? You are gifted in reading and writing—you must use those gifts for the glory of God."

"I can do that here, sir. No one else knows your translation the way I do."

"But—but what about your family, Seppel? Your mother and your sisters—do you not wish to return to them?"

I swallowed. "The other night when we were surrounded by enemies, as we thought, you ordered me to abandon you in order to preserve the Word of God. I obeyed you that night, sir. I understand what it means to leave behind those I love in order to serve God. I believe I have been called to serve here in Wittenberg. The printer offered me work, sir. He told me I have a good eye, and you know I have a neat hand."

Doctor Luther stared at his inkwell. Just as on that long-ago day at the Dragon's Gorge, I waited to learn whether my companion would respond with anger or disappointment or relief.

At last he looked up again. "Are you quite certain that this is the right decision?"

"I have put my hand to the plow, sir. I will not look back."

Doctor Luther said, "You are perhaps too adept a pupil." Then he smiled. "Very well, Seppel. Let us tell your uncle Spalatin that your place is here in the Kingdom of the Word."

Every morning for eight days Doctor Luther preached in the Town Church. Every afternoon I walked from Cranach House to the Black Cloister to copy the pages that he set out for me. Next I carried the finished pages to *Herr* Lotther, who appointed me a proofreader when the first pages came off the press.

My days and nights became a blur of black columns. Cranach and Doerring, who were financing the New Testament project, were so impatient to see the book in print that they supplied Lotther with a second press. I no longer had time to make fair copy, and while I missed the company of Doctor Luther, my work at the press was utterly absorbing. By July we had three presses running, each assigned a different section of the Scriptures.

On a sweltering day in August, Doctor Luther came to Cranach House to see me. I was eager to show him the latest proof sheets, but he gently brushed my work aside. "I have sobering news. Lady von Berlepsch has died. The captain asks us to remember his family in our prayers."

As we prayed, I thought of the deep-hollowed eyes, the gentle voice, and the pale blue-veined hands guiding mine on the strings of the lute. I had not thought of the family von Berlepsch or any of their servants in many weeks. Already that mountaintop castle seemed to belong to another life entirely.

"The captain also writes that Ilse is betrothed to Peter Custodomus." said Doctor Luther. "That young man has a fine voice and a good heart. I think our Ilse will be very happy."

A month later I hurried down Market Street with a package as precious as the contents of the saddlebag Tintenfleck had carried from the Wartburg. "Doctor Luther!" I called, my voice echoing in the corridors of the Black Cloister.

With great ceremony I set the newly bound book upon my friend's desk.

"*Gott sei dank.*" Slowly he lifted the cover and stared at the title page of the German New Testament. He turned a few pages, hardly seeming to see them. Then he picked up his quill and wrote on the flyleaf: To my host in the Kingdom of the Birds.

"Seppel, I believe Captain von Berlepsch will be very pleased to learn that our scribbling has amounted to something after all."

CHAPTER 33

Years After

Doctor Luther married less than three years after we left the
Wartburg. I remember his rueful smile when he told me he intended
to wed a runaway nun living at Cranach House. Katy von Bora was
a daughter of the nobility as strong-willed as Ilse von Berlepsch, but
she had a sweeter disposition. The Luthers set up housekeeping in the
Black Cloister, their wedding gift from Duke Frederick.

Much later, when I became partner in a print shop, I married a red-
haired niece of Christian Doerring. Doctor Luther was godfather to our
firstborn child, and for many years little Burkhardts romped with the
Luther children upstairs and down in the Black Cloister.

In old age Tintenfleck became quite fat, but he remained so good-
tempered that my boys and girls used to climb all over him and ride
bareback around the garden. Captain von Berlepsch would have been
dismayed at their lack of horsemanship. *"Bei allen Heiligen!"* I can
hear him say. "Is that a horse or a hay wagon?" At times my children
have to be reminded that *"Was sehrt, das lehrt."*

The household of the Wartburg has not been forgotten. On winter
nights when the Burkhardt family gathers around the fireplace to sing
in four parts and read the Scriptures, one of my little ones is sure to
point to the sword above the mantel and say, "Please, Papa, tell us
another story of the Kingdom of the Birds."

Author's Note

In May 1521, Wittenberg professor Martin Luther was captured by horsemen in the Thuringian Forest and taken to the Wartburg Castle. This abduction had been masterminded by Spalatin, chaplain to Duke Frederick of Saxony, the territorial lord and patron of Wittenberg University, in order to protect the outlawed professor from his enemies. Disguising Luther as a knight, Hans von Berlepsch, warden of the Wartburg, served as the outlaw's guardian for ten months. During this exile Luther corresponded frequently with friends and colleagues, at times referring to his hiding place as the "Kingdom of the Birds."

Martin Luther's letters from the Wartburg provided the framework for my story and inspired many scenes. The famous professor made a most unlikely knight, and Captain von Berlepsch must have struggled with the decision to permit Luther to make a winter journey to Wittenberg, where the outlaw met secretly with Philip Melanchthon and Nicholas Amsdorf and had his portrait painted by Lucas Cranach. Upon returning to the Wartburg, Luther began to translate the New Testament into German, a task that he finished in eleven weeks.

My imagination peopled the Wartburg with those who were influenced by encounters with Martin Luther. While Seppel and Ilse, Dame Adela, and the servants are my own inventions, I have lived with them so long that they seem as real as any figures in history.

Educational resources related to *Kingdom of the Birds* are available online at the website www.kingdomofthebirds.wordpress.com

Acknowledgments

Among my richest blessings I count my husband Mark P. Lutze and our children Katrina, Elena (also known as the literary assistant), and Matthew, who have endured years of my scribbling. I am grateful for the love and support of the Demuth and Lutze families, especially Marjorie and the late Robert Demuth, Karl and Gail Lutze, Emily Demuth Ishida, who inspired me to write about Martin Luther, and Gretchen M. D. Hansen, who assured me that my scribbling would amount to something after all.

I am indebted to Gottfried G. Krodel, esteemed mentor and dear friend, whose criticism and conversation refined my vision of Luther's world and helped to shape the story. Pastors Paul Bretscher and Don Williams were generous in loaning books from their personal collections, and at Valparaiso University both the old Moellering Library and the new Christopher Center proved hospitable places for research and writing.

Many thanks to Ed Uehling, who supervised an independent study on writing historical fiction, and to Arlin Meyer, Kathleen Mullen, Marliese Springsteen, Doug Pishkur, and Elizabeth Lynn for their responses to early chapters. Special thanks to faithful reader Dan Querry for his droll analysis of my work in progress. I appreciate the encouragement of longtime friends Don Driscoll, Rich Novotney, Jim Hale, JoAnn Campbell, and Brad Enslen, and I have benefited greatly from the insights of my fellow writers at Chesterton High School.

Selected Sources

Böcher, Otto. "Martin Luther und Hans von Berlepsch." *Genealogisches Jahrbuch.* Vol. 33/34. Neustadt a. d. Aisch, 1995.

Bornkamm, Heinrich. *Luther's World of Thought.* Trans. Martin H. Bertram. St. Louis: Concordia, 1958.

Brecht, Martin. *Martin Luther 1521-1532: Shaping and Defining the Reformation.* Trans. James L. Schaaf. Philadelphia: Fortress Press, 1990.

Höss, Irmgard. *Georg Spalatin, 1488-1545.* 2nd ed. Weimar, 1989.

Luther, Martin. *Luther's Works.* Vol. 48. Letters I. Trans./Ed. Gottfried G. Krodel. Philadelphia: Fortress Press, 1963.

_____. *Luther's Works.* Vol. 52. Sermons II. Ed. Hans J. Hillerbrand. Philadelphia: Fortress Press, 1974.

Ritgen, Hans von. *Der Führer auf der Wartburg: ein Wegweiser für Fremde und ein Beitrag zur Kunde der Vorzeit.* Leipzig: J. J. Weber, 1876.

Schaff, Philip. *History of the Christian Church.* Vol. 7. New York: Charles Scribner's Sons, 1907.

Schwiebert, E. G. *Luther and His Times.* St. Louis: Concordia, 1950.

Thulin, Oskar, Ed. *Illustrated History of the Reformation.* St. Louis: Concordia, 1967.

Todd, John M. *Luther: A Life.* New York: Crossroad Publishing, 1982.